WHO WILL SURVIVE?

IT'S GOING
TO BE A
KILLER
YEAR!

Is the senior class at Shadyside High doomed? That's the prediction Trisha Conrad makes at her summer party—and it looks as if she may be right. Spend a year with the Fear Street seniors, as each month in this new 12-book series brings horror after horror. Will anyone reach graduation day alive?

Only R.L. Stine knows...

SHADYSIDE HIGH YEARBOOK

Trisha Conrad

LIKES:
Shopping in the mall my dad owns, giving fabulous parties, Gary Fresno

REMEMBERS:
The murder game, the senior table at Pete's Pizza

HATES:
Rich girl jokes, bad karma, overalls

QUOTE:
"What you don't know will hurt you."

Clark Dickson

LIKES:
Debra Lake, poetry, painting

REMEMBERS:
Trisha's party, the first time I saw Debra

HATES:
Nicknames, dentists, garlic pizza, tans

QUOTE:
"Fangs for the memories."

Jennifer Fear

LIKES:
Basketball, antique jewelry, cool music

REMEMBERS:
The doom spell, senior cut day, hanging with Trisha and Josie

HATES:
The way people are afraid of the Fears, pierced eyebrows

QUOTE:
"There's nothing to fear but fear itself."

Jade Feldman

LIKES:
Cheerleading, expensive clothes, working out

REMEMBERS:
Ice cream and gab fests with Dana

HATES:
Cheerleading captains, ghosts, SAT prep courses

QUOTE:
"You get what you pay for."

Gary Fresno

LIKES:
Hanging out by the bleachers, art class, gym

REMEMBERS:
Cruisin' down Division Street with the guys, that special night with that special person (you know who you are...)

HATES:
My beat-up Civic, working after school everyday, cops

QUOTE:
"Don't judge a book by its cover."

Kenny Klein

LIKES:
Jade Feldman, chemistry, Latin, baseball

REMEMBERS:
The first time I beat Marla Newman in a debate, Junior Prom with Jade

HATES:
Nine-year-olds who like to torture camp counselors, cafeteria food

QUOTE:
"Look before you leap."

Debra Lake

LIKES:
Sensitive guys, tennis, Clark's poems

REMEMBERS:
Basketball games, when Clark painted my portrait

HATES:
Possessive boyfriends and jealous girlfriends

QUOTE:
"I would do anything for you, but I won't do that."

Stacy Malcolm

LIKES:
Sports, funky hats, shopping

REMEMBERS:
Running laps with Mary, stuffing our faces at Pete's, Mr. Morley and Rob

HATES:
Psycho killers, stealing boyfriends

QUOTE:
"College, here I come!"

Josh Maxwell

LIKES:
Debra Lake, Debra Lake, Debra Lake

REMEMBERS:
Hanging out at the old mill, senior camp-out, Coach's pep talks

HATES:
Funeral homes, driving my parents' car, tomato juice

QUOTE:
"Sometimes you don't realize the truth until it bites you right on the neck."

Josie Maxwell

LIKES:
Black clothes, black nail polish, black lipstick, photography

REMEMBERS:
Trisha's first senior party, the memorial wall

HATES:
Algebra, evil spirits (including Marla Newman), being compared to my stepbrother Josh

QUOTE:
"The past isn't always the past—sometimes it's the future."

Mickey Meyers

LIKES:
Jammin' with the band, partying, hot girls

REMEMBERS:
Swimming in Fear Lake, the storm, my first gig at the Underground

HATES:
Dweebs, studying, girls who diet, station wagons

QUOTE:
"Shadyside High rules!"

Marla Newman

LIKES:
Writing, cool clothes, being a redhead

REMEMBERS:
Yearbook deadlines, competing with Kenny Klein, when Josie put a spell on me (ha ha)

HATES:
Girls who wear all black, guys with long hair, the dark arts

QUOTE:
"The power is divided when the circle is not round."

Mary O'Connor

LIKES:
Running, ripped jeans, hair spray

REMEMBERS:
Not being invited to Trisha's party, rat poison

HATES:
Social studies, rich girls, cliques

QUOTE:
"Just say no."

Dana Palmer

LIKES:
Boys, boys, boys, cheerleading, short skirts

REMEMBERS:
Senior camp-out with Mickey, Homecoming, the back seat

HATES:
Private cheerleading performances, fire batons, sharing clothes

QUOTE:
"The bad twin always wins!"

Deidre Palmer

LIKES:
Mysterious guys, sharing clothes, old movies

REMEMBERS:
The cabin in the Fear Street woods, sleepovers at Jen's

HATES:
Being a "good girl," sweat socks

QUOTE:
"What you see isn't always what you get."

Will Reynolds

LIKES:
The Turner family, playing guitar, clubbing

REMEMBERS:
The first time Clarissa saw me without my dreads, our booth at Pete's

HATES:
Lite FM, the clinic, lilacs

QUOTE:
"I get knocked down, but I get up again..."

Ty Sullivan

LIKES:
Cheerleaders, waitresses, Fears, psychics, brains, football

REMEMBERS:
The graveyard with you know who, Kenny Klein's lucky shot

HATES:
Painting fences, Valentine's Day

QUOTE:
"The more the merrier."

Clarissa Turner

LIKES:
Art, music, talking on the phone

REMEMBERS:
Shopping with Debra, my first day back to school, eating pizza with Will

HATES:
Mira Block

QUOTE:
"Real friendship never dies."

Matty Winger

LIKES:
Computers, video games, Star Trek

REMEMBERS:
The murder game—good one Trisha

HATES:
People who can't take a joke, finding Clark's cape with Josh

QUOTE:
"Don't worry, be happy."

Phoebe Yamura

LIKES:
Cheerleading, gymnastics, big crowds

REMEMBERS:
That awesome game against Waynesbridge, senior trip, tailgate parties

HATES:
When people don't give it their all, liars, vans

QUOTE:
"Today is the first day of the rest of our lives."

episode two **In Too Deep**

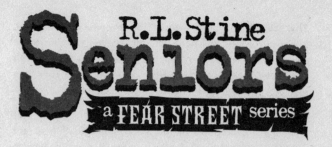

R.L. Stine
Seniors
a FEAR STREET series

episode two **In Too Deep**

A Parachute Press Book

A GOLD KEY PAPERBACK
Golden Books Publishing Company, Inc.
New York

A GOLD KEY Paperback Original

Golden Books Publishing Company, Inc.
888 Seventh Avenue
New York, NY 10106

ISBN: 0-307-24706-6

First Gold Key Paperback printing August 1998

10 9 8 7 6 5 4 3 2 1

Photography by Jimmy Levin

Printed in the U.S.A.

In Too Deep

Kenny Klein slid his arms around Jade Feldman and pulled her close. "I wish you didn't have to go," he murmured.

"*I* wish you could come with me." Jade kissed him and leaned her forehead against his chest. "Just think how much fun we could have in California together."

For a few seconds Kenny imagined the two of them on a beach somewhere in Southern California. Jade's long dark hair gleaming in the sun. Her skin all shiny with lotion . . . Jade wearing a spectacular bikini.

1

Yeah, right, he thought. It's not going to happen, so don't even think about it.

"It just isn't fair," Jade declared. "I mean, this is the summer before our senior year in high school. We're supposed to have fun and party a lot. And I have to spend a whole month taking an SAT-prep course."

"At least you'll be in California," Kenny told her. "I'll be stuck here in Shadyside serving bug juice to little kids."

Tomorrow Kenny started his summer job as a counselor at Shadyside Day Camp, where he would be in charge of a group of nine-year-old boys. "I hope I don't get a bunch of kids who hate me," he said with a sigh.

"Are you kidding? They'll be crazy about you, just like I am." Jade kissed him again.

Kenny kissed her back. Then he gazed over her shoulder into the front yard. It was a hot night in late June, with a bright moon and no wind. Perfect for a late-night swim in Fear Lake, he thought. The water was freezing, but so what? They could cuddle under a blanket together afterward. Too bad Jade's plane for California left at eight-thirty in the morning—her parents wanted her in early tonight.

As if on cue, the porch light flashed on.

Jade groaned softly. "I'll be in in one minute, Dad!" she called out.

Kenny sighed. He really hated saying good-bye.

"Promise me something, okay?" Jade asked, staring up at him. "Don't go getting interested in any other girls while I'm gone."

"How could I? The only girls I'll see will be about eight years old."

"I'm serious," Jade replied. "I want us to be together for all of our senior year, Kenny. Don't let anything or anyone come between us. Promise?"

"I promise," Kenny whispered, and kissed her good-bye.

Early the next morning Kenny parked his Jeep in the staff parking lot and joined the rest of the counselors in a big clearing in the middle of Shadyside Day Camp. Dana Palmer and Debra Lake, two girls from his class, spotted him and waved him over.

"Kenny, hi!" Debra cried. Short and thin, she wore the day camp uniform—khaki shorts and a yellow T-shirt. "Are you ready for the first day?"

"I guess." Kenny dropped his duffel bag onto the hard-packed dirt and glanced at his watch. Eight-forty. Jade's plane was probably taking off right now.

Dana tossed her long wavy blond hair and grinned at him. "So, did you and Jade have a really romantic last night together?"

Kenny shook his head. "Her dad practically dragged her inside at ten."

"Aww, don't look so sad," Dana teased. "You can talk to her every night on the telephone. Besides, just think how much fun you two will have when she gets back."

Kenny turned as Craig Sherman, the camp director, hurried into the clearing. He was about thirty, with close-cropped hair and an easygoing smile. "Morning, everybody. Welcome to Shadyside Day Camp. The buses are supposed to be here at nine, but they're always late on the first day. If anyone has any questions, now is the time to ask."

As Craig began to answer some questions, Kenny glanced around. A long low building at the edge of the clearing held Craig's office and the infirmary. Gravel paths led through pine trees to more buildings—the arts and crafts cabin, the recreation hall, the dining cabin, and a storage shed.

In the distance Kenny could see the ball field and the archery range. Behind him, another path led to small white cabins that each group of campers would use for rest periods and overnight stays. Beyond the cabins stood Fear Lake.

He'd missed the orientation Craig had held for the counselors. But it didn't matter. It looks exactly the same, Kenny thought, remembering the two summers he had spent here when he was eight and nine.

4

"Okay, guys," Craig called out. "Why don't you stow your duffel bags in your cabins, then take a walk around and reacquaint yourselves with the place before the kids arrive."

Kenny said good-bye to Dana and Debra, then picked up his bag. As he started down the trail toward Cabin Five, Craig called him over.

"I just wanted to remind you about that kid in your group," Craig told him quietly. "Take it easy with him. He's troubled, remember?"

A troubled kid? All Kenny remembered about his group was that they were nine years old. What did *troubled* mean? he wondered uneasily. Did the kid freak out and have fits or something? Kenny wasn't sure he could handle that.

"You read those camper profiles I mailed to you, right?" Craig asked.

Kenny hesitated. He had received a fat envelope from the camp. He'd been in a hurry, so he'd barely glanced inside. When he tried to find it a few days later, it had disappeared. Probably recycled with the newspapers.

"Uh . . . the profiles. Sure," he said. "I read them."

Great, he thought. Start the job with a lie.

"Good. Just wanted to remind you." Craig clapped him on the shoulder again. He handed Kenny a name tag, then hurried off to the office.

Yawning, Kenny stuck the name tag on his T-shirt and strolled down one of the paths to the campers' cabins. All of them had numbers carved out of wood hanging over the doors. He stepped into Cabin 5 and glanced around. Shadyside Day Camp had overnighters once a week, so bunk beds lined the walls. A green-shaded lightbulb hung from the middle of the ceiling. Kenny tossed his duffel bag in a corner and went back outside.

Another path led to a clearing where a guy dressed in khaki and yellow was hanging tetherballs on their poles. He looked about Kenny's age. "Hey," Kenny called out. "Need any help?"

The guy glanced over. Tall and muscular, he wore his blond hair in a buzz cut and had a small gold ring in his left eyebrow. "No, thanks. This is the last one." He eyed Kenny's shorts and yellow shirt. "You're a counselor, too, huh?"

Kenny nodded and introduced himself.

"Tyler Sullivan. Call me Ty," the guy said. "Hey, do you go to Shadyside High? I'm transferring there from a private school in September."

Kenny nodded. "I'll be a senior."

"Me, too, and I can't wait. There weren't any girls in my other school." He smirked as Kenny stifled another yawn. "Late night out?"

"Not really. I just couldn't sleep." Kenny had been thinking of Jade, missing her the minute he left her house.

"Don't snooze on this job," Ty warned him. "The kids love to play tricks on the counselors."

He quickly pulled the tetherball back and swung it toward Kenny. "You have to stay on your toes!"

Kenny barely had time to duck. Ty grabbed the ball and swung it again. This time Kenny leaped up and batted it back. For a few minutes they batted the ball around the pole, working up a sweat in the morning sun.

A few other counselors stopped and began to cheer them on. Kenny was enjoying himself—until he caught the expression on Ty's face. Ty's jaw was clenched and his eyes were narrowed, glinting fiercely.

Whoa, Kenny thought. This isn't a game to him. It's war.

"You ready to call it quits?" Ty challenged. "You can't win. Might as well give up now!"

Kenny shook his head. As the ball sailed toward him, he grabbed it and punched it hard—straight into Ty's face.

"YAAIII!" Ty staggered backward, pressing his hands over his nose. Blood gushed from between his fingers.

"Oh, man, I'm sorry!" Kenny cried. He patted the pockets of his shorts and pulled out the packet of tissues his mother had made him bring in case a camper needed one. "Here," he said, holding them out. "Are you okay?"

Ty angrily punched the packet out of Kenny's hand. "Yeah. Great."

"Hey, I'm sorry," Kenny repeated. "It was an accident."

Ty wiped his nose, but the blood kept streaming out. "No such thing as *accidents*," he said.

Kenny glanced around. The other counselors were all staring at him. He turned back to Ty. "You have to be kidding. You really think I did that on purpose?"

"Forget it." Ty pointed a bloody finger at Kenny. "Just watch yourself, understand?"

As Ty stalked toward the infirmary building, Kenny stared after him, shocked. What's his problem? he wondered.

Then he sighed and began ambling down the trail leading to the lake. First I lie to my boss, he thought. Then I get into a fight with another counselor. What's next?

Halfway to the lake, Kenny stopped.

A girl in tan shorts and a yellow shirt stood on the sandy shore, gazing out at the rippling gray water. A breeze blew her long, pale blond hair back from her face. Even from this distance, Kenny could see that she was beautiful.

As he watched, the girl turned and began to walk along the water's edge.

She's not walking, Kenny thought. She's drifting. Floating along the shore.

She can't be real, Kenny told himself. She's too beautiful. I must be imagining her. If I blink, she'll probably disappear.

Kenny squeezed his eyes shut for half a second, then snapped them open.

Fear Lake stretched out in front of him, sparkling in the sun.

And the girl had vanished.

Chapter TWO

Kenny gasped. I don't believe it!

He shut his eyes and counted to five.

When he opened them, he let his breath out in relief.

The girl had reappeared. She stood near the shore, clutching a handful of bright blue wild-flowers.

She just ducked down to pick some flowers, dummy, Kenny told himself.

You didn't dream her up. She's real.

And she's beautiful.

Kenny started down the trail, keeping an eye on the girl as he crunched noisily over the pebbles. She stuck a couple of flowers into her hair, then turned and stared out at the lake again.

"Hi," Kenny called out as he drew closer.

The girl didn't move.

"Hi!" he called again, louder this time.

She gasped and spun around, dropping the rest of the flowers.

"Sorry," Kenny said. "Did I scare you? I didn't mean to."

"That's okay." She bent down toward the flowers.

"Let me get those," Kenny said quickly. He snatched them up and held them out.

"Thanks." The girl straightened up and took them. Their fingers brushed.

Kenny felt his heartbeat double. Her eyes were spectacular. Big and green. Dark green, like the leaves on the wildflowers.

But they were filled with tears.

"I . . . I'm sorry," Kenny stammered. "Are you crying?"

"What? No," she said quickly. "I'm allergic to the flowers, that's all." A tear rolled down her cheek. She brushed it away and laughed softly. "I just couldn't resist them, they're so beautiful."

"Yeah." Like you, Kenny thought.

"Here. You take them." She stepped close and tucked the flowers into the pocket on Kenny's T-shirt.

"What's your name?" he asked.

"Melly."

"Mine's Kenny," he told her. He stared into her eyes and swallowed. "I saw you before, walking

11

along the lake. Are you the waterfront counselor?"

Melly gasped and stepped back, shaking her head.

"What's wrong?" Kenny asked. "What did I say?"

"Nothing!" Melly covered her nose and sneezed three times in a row.

Kenny laughed. "I think you'd better take those flowers out of your hair."

"I guess you're right." She pulled the blue flowers out and tossed them into the lake. "Anyway, I'm not the waterfront counselor," she said. "I'm arts and crafts. What about you?"

"I have a group of nine-year-old boys." Kenny rolled his eyes. "I think I'm in major trouble. When I was nine, I was a beast!"

"You?" Melly shook her head. "I don't believe it. You're much too nice."

"Yeah, well . . ." Kenny's heart sped up again. He felt about twelve, having his first major crush on a girl. "I still expect to see a group of monsters come stampeding toward me when the buses arrive."

"I'll bet they really like you," Melly told him. "After all, I just met you, and *I* like you." She touched his arm. "Don't worry about *them*. It's Tyler you should watch out for," she whispered.

"Huh? Ty?" Kenny ran a hand through his sandy hair. "I already met him."

Melly's expression grew hard. "Watch out for him," she repeated. "He's really cold."

"Yeah, he's definitely got an attitude," Kenny agreed.

"It's worse than that," Melly insisted. "He has a real cruel streak. Be careful, Kenny."

Kenny shrugged. "Come on, I don't think—"

"I mean it," Melly whispered. "I know what I'm talking about!"

Kenny narrowed his eyes at her. "You know him? You've been here before?"

"Yes," Melly replied softly. "Before I drowned."

Chapter Three

"Huh? What did you say?" Kenny asked, startled. "Until you drowned?"

Melly giggled. "No. I said until I left *town*." She gave him a playful shove. "Maybe you're allergic to those flowers, too. Maybe they affect your hearing!"

"Yeah, maybe." Kenny laughed, too, embarrassed. He suddenly wished she would wrap her arms around his neck and kiss him.

Get a grip, he told himself. You just met her. Last night you promised Jade you wouldn't even look at any other girls.

But that was last night, he thought. Jade is halfway to California by now.

And Melly is right here, staring at me with those big green eyes. Teasing me. Flirting with me.

14

Can I really keep that promise to Jade?

Melly pulled the flowers out of Kenny's pocket and tossed them into the lake. Then she stood on tiptoe and brought her lips close to his ear. "See if you can hear me now," she whispered. "Would you like to take a walk along the shore?"

Definitely! Kenny thought. But before he could say it, a loud whistle pierced the air. Turning, he saw Craig standing at the top of the path, waving at them to come up.

"Lousy timing," Kenny grumbled as he and Melly started up the path.

"Don't worry," Melly assured him. "We'll have plenty of time together." She squeezed his arm. "I'll make sure of it."

Whoa! Kenny thought. She's really coming on to me. That promise to Jade will *not* be easy to keep!

"Ty needs some help over by the storage shed," Craig said as the three of them walked back to camp. "He's having trouble with some equipment, and I have to go over a bunch of paperwork before the campers arrive." He hurried to the office.

Kenny turned to Melly. "See you later?"

"Promise." Melly started jogging toward the arts and crafts cabin.

Kenny jumped as someone touched his arm.

Dana stood next to him, shaking her head and clicking her tongue. "It's a good thing Jade's not here," she teased. "She definitely wouldn't like the way you're staring at that girl. What's her name, anyway?"

"Melly." Kenny felt his face flush. "And I wasn't staring."

"You could have fooled me." Dana laughed and ran off toward the main clearing.

Better be careful, Kenny told himself. Dana is on the cheerleading squad with Jade. She might tell her about Melly. Not that there's anything to tell.

Not yet, anyway.

Stuffing his hands in his pockets, Kenny followed the path toward the storage shed. As he reached it, he heard a shout.

Ty stood in front of a large wooden trunk, his hands on his hips and a scowl on his face. The lid stood open, nets and balls and ropes spilling out of the trunk.

Ty's face turned red with anger. He pounded the trunk with his fists, then gave it a kick.

The guy is definitely having a bad day, Kenny told himself. He cleared his throat. "Uh, Craig asked me to give you a hand."

Ty glanced up. His scowl deepened. "You," he muttered coldly.

Kenny walked over and checked out the trunk. "Think we should unpack the whole thing and start again?" he asked.

"No way. I've got other things to do." Ty took

out three volleyballs, then pulled out the net. "Let's fold this up better. See if that helps."

"Sure." Kenny began helping him untangle the net. "How come you're putting it all away?"

"Don't ask me," Ty grumbled. "First Craig tells me to take out the volleyball equipment. Then he tells me to put it back. I just follow orders."

"Yeah. Bosses can be a pain, right?" Kenny asked.

Ty didn't respond.

Okay, he's not going to loosen up, Kenny decided. So don't even bother to talk. Just get the job done.

In silence, Kenny helped fold the net as flat and small as possible. He stuffed it into the bottom of the trunk and stood aside as Ty placed the three volleyballs on top.

"Okay, let's shut this thing," Ty muttered. He grabbed the lid and pulled it down.

It almost closed, but not quite.

Ty uttered an angry curse.

He's going to go ballistic again, Kenny saw. He quickly lifted the lid and shifted the balls around. "Let's try shutting it together," he suggested. "Count of three."

Ty muttered something under his breath and grabbed hold of the lid.

"One . . . two . . ." Out of the corner of his eye, Kenny caught a glimpse of a girl with long, pale blond hair. He shifted his gaze.

Melly waved at him as she walked past.

"Three!" Kenny shouted—and slammed the lid down as hard as he could.

Kenny heard a sickening crack.

He gasped as Ty shrieked in fury. "My hand! You *broke* my hand!"

Chapter Four

Kenny froze in horror. The cracking sound—
the sound of breaking bones—repeated in
his ears.

"Get the lid off!" Ty wailed. "Ohhh, man!"
Kenny shoved the lid up.

Ty's hand turned a fiery red as the blood
rushed into it. Sucking air through his teeth, he
pulled it away and hugged it against his chest.

"I'm sorry!" Kenny choked out. "I didn't see . . .
I mean . . . come on, let's get to the infirmary."

As they hurried down the path, Ty walked
hunched over, protecting his hand. His face was
pale and his breath came in quick little gasps.

"I'm really sorry," Kenny repeated. "I don't
know what happened." Actually, he did. The second he saw Melly, everything else flew out of his

mind. You're losing it, he told himself. Fast!

Ty scowled at him. "You broke my hand, that's what happened. Before that, you messed up my nose. What's next on your list—my *neck*?"

Kenny wanted to argue that it was an accident. But Ty was obviously in horrible pain. Kenny decided to keep his mouth shut.

As they entered the main building, Craig stepped out of his office into the hallway. "Accident?" he asked, eyeing Ty's hand. "How bad is it?"

"Bad," Ty muttered. Still hunched over, he hurried down the hall to the infirmary. "And it was no accident!" he shouted over his shoulder.

Craig turned to Kenny and raised his eyebrows. "What happened?"

Kenny took a deep breath. "I slammed the trunk lid on his hand," he explained. "He has this idea that I did it on purpose. But that's crazy. Why would I? I don't even know him."

"Let it drop," Craig said. "Ty is a little hot-tempered."

"No kidding," Kenny agreed.

"He's hurting right now, so he isn't thinking clearly," Craig reminded him. "Once the pain stops, he'll realize you didn't mean to do it."

I'm not so sure about that, Kenny thought.

"Come on," Craig said. "Let's go see how he's doing."

Kenny reluctantly followed Craig down the hall

to the nurse's office. Inside, Ty sat on a chair, cradling his hand in a soft ice pack.

The nurse stood at the desk talking on the telephone. She hung up just as Kenny and Craig came in.

"What's the diagnosis, Mrs. Gomez?" Craig asked.

"It might be broken, but we don't have the equipment to find out." Mrs. Gomez blew a wisp of black hair off her forehead. "I just called the ambulance. They'll take Ty to Shadyside General for an X-ray. Then we'll know for sure."

"I already know," Ty declared. "It's broken."

"Let's hope not," Craig told him. "If it is, you might not be able to be a counselor this summer."

Ty snapped his head up. "But I need this job! You can't fire me just because I'm hurt!"

"Ty, you're a swimming instructor," Craig reminded him. "If your hand is broken . . ."

Ty lowered his head unhappily. "But,—" he started to protest.

"Let's wait and find out what shows up on the X-rays," Craig said, patting Ty on the shoulder. He turned to Kenny. "You'd better get outside. The buses will be here in just a few minutes."

Kenny nodded. He opened his mouth to say something to Ty. But he stopped when he saw Ty's hateful expression. This is your fault, he seemed to be saying. And I'll make you pay.

Kenny turned away, shaken. Forget about apologizing, he thought. Ty will never forgive me. And he'll never forget.

Outside the infirmary building, Kenny took a deep breath of fresh air. Then he began walking toward the big open space where the buses would pull up. He spotted Melly a little way ahead of him and ran to catch up.

"Kenny!" she cried, spinning around and grabbing his arm. "Is everything okay?"

"Not really," he replied. "The guy's hand might be broken, and he blames me. Looks like I've made an enemy."

"That's not fair. I saw the whole thing," she declared. "It wasn't your fault."

"Try telling him that." Kenny shook his head. "You warned me about Ty. Now I'm really on his bad side."

"Wait a minute!" Melly stared at him. "Did that guy tell you his name was Ty?"

Kenny frowned. "Sure. What do you mean?"

"He isn't Ty," Melly said. "He doesn't look anything like Ty!"

Chapter Five

Kenny stared at her. "What do you mean?"

As Melly started to reply, a horn honked loudly. "It's the buses!" she cried.

"Wait a sec. What did you mean about Ty?" Kenny demanded.

A second horn blasted the air, and Craig came jogging down the path. "Show time!" he called out.

"I'll see you later." Melly turned and dashed away.

Kenny ran a hand through his hair and checked to make sure his name tag was still stuck to the front of his shirt. Then he hurried down the trail to the big open area.

Dana and Debra called to him when he arrived. Kenny waved and started walking toward them.

But before he reached them, three yellow buses pulled to a stop in the turnaround drive.

The bus doors opened and kids began tumbling out. Squeals and shouts filled the air as they stepped into the clearing. They carried backpacks and wore tags with their names and a number on a rope around their necks.

Craig blew a whistle. "Okay, people! Settle down!" he shouted. "Let's get you matched up with your counselors!"

The noise died down a little.

"Girl's group number one!" Craig called out. "All girls with a one on their name tag—over here!"

Debra Lake gathered the group together. As she began checking their names off on a list, Craig called for boys' group number one.

Ten minutes later Kenny's group was called. He pulled his list of names from his pocket as several nine-year-old boys gathered around him. "Hey, guys, I'm Kenny."

"Well, duh," one of them said. He was a chunky kid, with red hair and a chubby freckled face. He pointed at Kenny's name tag and snickered. "You think we can't read?"

Great, Kenny thought. A smart mouth. He checked the kid's name against his list—Graydon Boyce. Then he went on to the next. Dan, David, Matthew, Charlie and Simon. One was missing—Vincent.

"Stay right here," Kenny told the group. He

trotted over to Craig and told him about the missing kid.

"He must be around somewhere," Craig said. "Maybe his parents are bringing him. I'll check."

"Hey!"

Kenny heard a shout. He turned in time to see Graydon give Charlie a shove that sent the wiry, dark-haired boy sprawling in the dirt.

The other boys scattered as Charlie scrambled up and rushed at Graydon. Graydon raised his fists.

"Okay, okay! Cut it out!" Kenny shouted. He stepped between the two boys and held them at arm's length. "What's the problem?"

"They both wanted to be first in line," Simon reported. He rolled his eyes. "Like being first is such a big deal."

"Who said anything about getting in line?" Kenny asked. "Anyway, Simon's right. Lining up *isn't* a big deal in our group. As long as you don't wander off or crash into each other, I don't care how you walk."

"Yeah, okay." Graydon shook off Kenny's hand and picked up his backpack.

"Okay, Charlie?" Kenny asked.

Charlie shot Graydon a dirty look. "Okay," he mumbled.

As Kenny began to tell the group about the day's activities, Craig appeared and pulled him aside. "I found Vincent," he said. "The poor kid was hiding behind one of the buses."

"Hiding? Why?" Kenny asked.

Craig lowered his voice.

"He wears a ski mask."

Kenny stared at him. "Huh?"

"To cover his face," Craig explained. "You read Vincent's profile. You know about the accident."

"Oh, right. Of course," Kenny said.

He felt a flicker of nervousness. Vincent must be the troubled one, he thought. The accident probably messed up his head, too.

"Try not to let your other kids make a big deal out of the mask," Craig went on. "I'm not sure Vincent could take it."

Kenny nodded uneasily.

"He's still by the buses," Craig said. "I'll go get him."

Craig trotted off, and Kenny turned to his group. He told them about Vincent. Just about the mask, though. Not that he was a troubled kid. "I'm counting on you guys to make him feel at home," he said. "I know you'll be nice to him."

"Why can't we have a *cool* group?" Graydon complained. "Why are we stuck with a freak?"

"You're a freak, too, *lard boy*. So why don't you just shut up?" Charlie shot back.

Graydon let out a roar and charged toward Charlie. Kenny grabbed his arm and pulled him back.

"Let go!" Graydon screamed. "You heard what he called me!"

"Yeah, and I heard what you called Vincent." Kenny dropped Graydon's arm. "Rule number one," he announced. "No name-calling. Call someone a name and you lose points."

"Points for what?" Matthew asked.

Kenny had no idea. He'd just made it up. Fortunately, Craig arrived with Vincent, and he didn't have to answer.

"Here he is," Craig announced in a cheerful tone. He patted Vincent on the shoulder and hurried off to talk to another group of campers.

Kenny gazed at the new boy. Small and skinny. He wore denim shorts, a loose white T-shirt, and sneakers.

Normal kid, Kenny thought. Yeah, right. Normal—except for the red-and-white ski mask covering his head and neck.

I wonder what it looks like under that mask, Kenny thought. The poor kid must be really messed up.

Vincent gazed at the rest of the campers. All Kenny could see of his face were his mouth and his blue eyes. Vincent chewed his bottom lip and blinked nervously.

I bet he gets teased like crazy, Kenny thought. Or totally ignored. No wonder he's troubled. Vincent locked his eyes onto Kenny. The boy adjusted his mask and gave Kenny a little grin.

The mask gave Kenny the creeps, but he felt kind of sorry for the kid. I have to be really nice to him, he decided. Pay attention to him.

Graydon took a step toward Vincent. Kenny held his breath. Here it comes, he thought. Graydon is going to shoot off his big mouth.

Graydon stared at Vincent's mask for a second. "Isn't it hot inside that thing?" he asked.

Kenny let his breath out. At least he didn't call him a freak.

Vincent hesitated. "Kind of," he replied in a soft, shy voice. "But it's not too bad."

Graydon kept eyeing the mask.

Before Graydon got the bright idea to rip it off, Kenny clapped his hands. "Okay, everybody, let's go to the cabin so you can stash your backpacks. Then we can explore this place."

Graydon and Charlie burst away, making a race out of the whole thing. The rest of the group followed in a clump, except for Vincent.

Vincent walked next to Kenny. Every time Kenny glanced over, he caught the kid staring up at him out of the eyeholes of the mask.

Vincent never looked away. The kid didn't even *blink*.

Kenny's uneasiness grew stronger. The sharp, watchful look in those blue eyes gave him a chill.

When they reached the cabin, Kenny assigned them their bunks, then took them back outside. They met Dana and her group of eleven-year-old girls on one of the paths. "How's it going?" Dana asked.

"Not too bad." Kenny glanced over his shoulder at Vincent. The boy stood apart from the others, watching him. Kenny shivered.

"What's with the ski mask?" Dana whispered, following Kenny's gaze.

"I'll tell you later," he murmured. "Let's just say I wish it didn't have any eyeholes. Then he couldn't keep staring at me."

Kenny herded his group on a quick tour around the camp. He pointed out the recreation building, the arts-and-crafts cabin, the infirmary, and the ball field.

Vincent kept close to Kenny the whole time. Always watching him. Don't let it get to you, Kenny told himself, trying to shake off the creepy feeling. He's just a kid.

They started back to the cabin, taking a hilly, roundabout nature trail through the woods.

"I'm bored," Dan griped.

"Me, too," Charlie agreed. "When can we swim in the lake?"

Kenny checked his clipboard. "We're not scheduled to swim for another half hour."

"Check *that* out," he added, pointing toward a dark opening in the hillside a few feet away. "I think it's a cave."

"It is!" Vincent cried. "Wow!"

Everyone stared at Vincent, startled. It was only the second time he'd spoken.

"That is so cool!" Vincent exclaimed.

Before Kenny could stop him, he scrambled between the boulders at the cave's entrance, pushed aside some vines, and disappeared inside.

As the other boys hurried to catch up, Kenny shouted at them to stop.

"*He* went in," Charlie argued. "Why can't we?"

"Because," Kenny said, "it might not be—"

A high-pitched wail of horror stopped him.

Was it coming from inside the cave?

Yes.

"Bats! The bats!" he heard Vincent shriek in terror. "Help! They've got me! Let go! Let go!"

Chapter Six

"**S**o what happened?" Josh Maxwell asked.
"You won't believe it," Kenny replied.
He popped a slice of pepperoni into his
mouth and gazed around the table.

Debra, Dana, Josh, and Mickey Myers had met
him at Pete's Pizza that night. Kenny noticed that
Josh kept glancing at Debra. He must feel weird
hanging out, now that Debra's with Clark
Dickson, Kenny thought.

Mickey slung an arm around Dana's shoulder.
"Okay, Kenny, stop chewing and tell us what happened."

Kenny swallowed and finished telling the story
of Vincent and the bats. "Vincent shot out of the
cave and ran screaming back to the cabin. One of
the counselors ran after him. My whole group

31

was really freaked. But I had to leave them and go check out the cave."

"And was it crawling with bats?" Dana asked, shivering.

Kenny shook his head. "No way. No bats. I looked around by the opening. The cave was empty."

"You're kidding," Josh said. "What scared the kid?"

"Nothing," Kenny replied. "Craig and I talked about it later, and we decided Vincent was just trying to get attention."

Mickey snorted. "It sounds like he gets enough already, with that ski mask."

"Poor little guy," Debra murmured.

"He sounds kind of weird to me," Dana declared.

"Yeah. The accident messed up more than his face, I guess," Kenny agreed. "I feel for him. But I don't know anything about how to handle a disturbed kid."

"Well, speaking of disturbed, I have some news about Mary O'Connor," Dana declared. "This is unbelievable. She got caught shoplifting at the mall."

"Whoa!" Debra cried.

"Earrings and and a pair of jeans," Dana said.

"I can't believe it!" Debra exclaimed. "She's so shy and quiet."

"You can be shy and quiet and still be a klepto," Mickey added.

"Is she still seeing Gary Fresno?" Dana asked.

Debra shrugged. "If she is, it won't be for long. He's been spending a lot of time with Trisha Conrad. You should have seen them together at Trisha's party."

"Can you believe Trisha's still saying that the senior class is going to die?" Josh piped in.

Mickey laughed. "Yeah right! And she probably believes all the stuff she sees on *The X Files,* too."

Kenny heard a soft cough and glanced up. Josie, Josh's stepsister, stood at the table. She wore a Pete's Pizza uniform—black jeans, red shirt, and a small red cap perched on top of her head.

Mickey snickered. "Hey, Josie, lose the hat. It looks like a mushroom growing out of your head."

"Give me a break." Josie set the check down on the table. "You guys are finished, aren't you?"

Mickey grabbed the check and pretended to inspect it. "Are you sure you added this up right? I know you got a D in math."

"Mickey, don't give me a hard time," Josie pleaded. "This is my first night on the job."

Josh snatched the check out of Mickey's hand. "He can't help it, Josie. He's disturbed."

"We're all disturbed," Mickey declared.

Josie frowned and hurried off to another table.

Kenny popped the last piece of crust into his mouth and glanced around the restaurant. A girl with light blond hair stood at the takeout counter, waiting for her order.

Melly?

The girl shifted her weight and gazed out over the tables. She didn't recognize him. Disappointed, he turned back to his friends. "Debra, you know Melly Baker, don't you? The arts and crafts counselor?"

Debra shook her head. "Not really. I only met her today."

"Me, too," Kenny said. "She told me she used to live in Shadyside."

Dana glanced at him curiously. "So?"

"Nothing. I just wondered if anybody knew her," Kenny replied, trying to sound casual.

"What does she look like?" Mickey asked.

"Blond hair and green eyes," Debra replied. "Pretty."

"*Very* pretty. Isn't she, Kenny?" Dana teased.

Kenny faked a laugh, as if he didn't care. But he felt his face get hot.

I should never have asked about Melly, he told himself. Dana's kidding now. But if she really gets suspicious. . . . He decided to change the subject. "Anybody want to see a movie?"

Mickey groaned. "Nothing good is playing." But then his eyes lit up. "I have a better idea. Why don't we go swimming in Fear Lake?"

"Excellent!" Dana agreed. "No little campers screaming and splashing around."

Debra shook her head. "Can't go. I'm meeting Clark." She shot Josh a quick glance.

Kenny winced. That's got to hurt. Josh still *likes* Debra.

"A swim sounds good to me," Josh said. "What about it, Kenny?"

Kenny hesitated. But only for a few seconds. Jade was gone and he didn't want to spend the night thinking about her. Or about Melly. "Sure," he agreed. "Let's go. What can happen?"

Kenny broke the surface with a gasp. He slicked water off his face and hair and glanced around.

"How is it?" Josh called. He was wading near the shore.

"Feels great!" Kenny shouted.

"Are you kidding? It's freezing!" Dana cried. She sat on top of Mickey's shoulders, clutching his hair as he moved waist-deep into the lake. "Why do you think I'm sitting up here?"

"It's not that cold," Mickey told her. "Check it out!" He pushed Dana's legs up and tumbled her backward into the water. Dana came up gasping, then tried to dunk him.

Kenny plunged forward, swimming hard to warm himself up. He rolled onto his back and floated for a minute, then straightened up and began to tread water. He glanced down the shore-line. Josh was still wading. Dana squealed as

Mickey tossed her off his shoulders again.

Kenny turned. Someone stood alone near the lake's edge. A girl in a white swimsuit, with long pale hair shining in the moonlight.

Melly.

Kenny felt a rush of excitement. He began swimming again, pulling himself toward Melly with long, powerful strokes. "I didn't expect to see you here," he declared breathlessly as he swam through the shallow water, and then stepped up beside her.

Melly gestured toward the lake. "It's such a beautiful night, I couldn't resist going for a swim." She reached up and brushed some drops of water from his face. Then she dropped her hand to his shoulder and left it there. "I've been thinking about you all day, Kenny."

Kenny took a slow breath. "Me too," he murmured.

Melly rose to her tiptoes and kissed him. First on the cheek, then on the mouth.

Kenny wrapped his arms around her waist and kissed her back.

"You're soaking wet!" Melly protested. But she didn't pull away.

Kenny kissed her again. This is unreal, he thought. I just met her this morning. But who cares? She's fantastic.

They kissed some more, then Melly pulled back and took Kenny's hand. "Come on. Let's go in the water."

Kenny turned toward the lake, but Melly tugged him back. "Not here," she told him. "I know a better place. Come on."

Holding hands, they strolled to a bend in the shoreline where a huge, high boulder jutted way out into the water. Motioning for Kenny to follow, Melly scrambled easily to the top.

"Can you take a dare?" she asked as she held out a hand and pulled Kenny up beside her.

"I don't know. What do you have in mind?"

"A high dive," she declared.

Kenny curled his toes around the lip of the boulder and peered down. Several smaller rocks were piled close against its base. Beyond them, the water looked dark and deep.

But is it deep enough to dive into? Kenny wondered.

"Well?" Melly asked. "I dare you to dive from here."

Kenny hesitated. We could kill ourselves on the rocks, he thought. Why does she want to do this? Kenny focused on the icy calm water below. But if I *don't* do it, she'll think I'm a wimp.

"I have a better idea," he told her. "We go together. Only we go feet first."

She made a face.

"Feet first," he insisted. He shivered. Was he about to break both legs? This is insane!

Melly shrugged. Her eyes flashed. "Okay. Let's do it. On the count of three?"

"Right." Kenny let go of Melly and bent his knees so he could spring out as far as possible.

"One!" Melly called.

Kenny glanced to his right. He could see his friends in the distance, talking together at the edge of the lake.

"Two!" Melly cried.

Kenny waved, but he wasn't sure if anyone saw him.

"Ready?" Melly asked.

"Sure."

"Good. You call it," she told him.

Kenny sucked in a breath. "Three!" he shouted, and leaped into the air.

Chapter Seven

K enny screamed all the way down. He slammed sideways into the dark water.

At least it's deep enough, he thought as he plunged down.

And then a horrible pain exploded in his head.

A rock! he thought. Did I hit a rock?

Dizzy and disoriented, Kenny tumbled through in the dark water, trying to find the surface. His ribs ached. His head throbbed.

Don't scream, he told himself. Don't breathe! Not yet!

But his lungs began to ache for air. Kenny couldn't hold his breath much longer. Was he headed in the right direction? Kenny couldn't tell.

Then he felt someone grab his arm.

Melly, he thought. Thank goodness she's okay. Thank goodness she's here!

Strong hands pulled him to the surface.

Kenny glimpsed Josh's frightened face. And Mickey, reaching for him. He heard Dana screaming. Choking, sputtering, Kenny dragged in breath after breath of air. Mickey grabbed him around the chest and towed him to the shore.

"What kind of dumb stunt was that?" Josh shouted.

"Don't yell at him!" Dana cried. "Can't you see his head is bleeding? He might have a concussion."

"You can't get a concussion if you don't have a brain," Mickey replied. "And nobody with a brain would jump off that rock."

"We thought you were going to drown." Dana sighed, dropping to her knees beside Kenny.

"So did I," Kenny choked out. His head pounded and his ribs still ached. "Thanks, everybody. Thanks, Melly."

"Who?" Josh stared at him, confused.

"Melly," Kenny uttered. He sat up. "We jumped off the rock together. Where is she?"

"Maybe you *can* get a concussion without a brain," Mickey said.

Kenny frowned. "What's that supposed to mean?"

"It means your head's out of whack," Mickey told him. "Nobody jumped off that rock but you."

"What are you talking about?" Kenny leaped to his feet and gazed around the shoreline. He stared up at the boulder, then out into Fear Lake. Nothing broke the rippling surface of the moonlit water.

"Melly!" Kenny screamed. "Melly!"

"Kenny, stop it! You were the only one who jumped off that rock!" Dana insisted.

"Yeah," Mickey agreed. "We heard you shout, and saw you push off. Alone."

"Are you guys blind?" Kenny shouted. "Melly had on a white swimsuit. How could you *not* see her?"

They all shook their heads.

"Then she must have gone under!" Kenny stared back out at the water, his heart pounding in panic. "We have to find her!"

Kenny started to run, but Mickey grabbed his arm and yanked him back. Kenny tried to wrench his arm free, but Mickey held on.

"What's the matter with you?" Kenny screamed, struggling frantically to break loose. "Don't you get it? I have to find her! I have to find Melly!"

"You're not thinking clearly," Mickey insisted. He tightened his grip.

"Come on, Kenny," Dana said. "Your head is bleeding. You're in shock or something."

Kenny struggled for a moment, but his friends held him back. Finally he grew too weak to fight them. He slumped onto the sand, dizzy and sick to his stomach. They don't believe me, he thought, gazing at their worried expressions. They think I hit my head so hard I just imagined that Melly was with me.

But I didn't.

She was there.

And now she's gone.

Kenny arrived at Shadyside Day Camp a few minutes early the next morning and hurried to the office. His ribs didn't ache anymore. Neither did his head. The cut had stopped bleeding long before he got home. He felt fine.

Except that he hadn't slept all night, worrying about Melly.

He'd listened to the all-news radio station on the way to camp, expecting to hear about a body found washed up on the shore of Fear Lake. But there had been nothing.

Did Melly drown or not? If she was okay, then why didn't she come back?

Was her body lying somewhere at the bottom of the lake?

Shuddering at the thought, Kenny darted into the office building and burst through Craig's door.

"Hey, watch it!" Ty leaped back as the door banged against the wall. His eyes narrowed in anger when he saw Kenny. "I should have known it was you. What's the matter? Haven't you done enough damage?" He held up his right hand, fitted in a splint and wrapped with gauze.

"Have you heard anything about Melly?" Kenny demanded, ignoring the hand. "Do you know what happened to her?"

"Huh? Melly?" Ty shook his head. "She gave me the evil eye when she saw me this morning. Don't ask me why."

Kenny felt a surge of hope. "You saw her this morning? Are you sure?"

"Sure I'm sure," Ty snapped. "You smashed my hand. But you didn't put my eyes out. Not yet, anyway."

Kenny breathed deeply, feeling totally relieved. "So she's okay?"

Ty shrugged. "I guess. She looked the same to me." He picked up the swimming schedule from Craig's desk and began reading it.

"Craig didn't fire you, huh?" Kenny asked.

"Obviously. He decided he could use me, even with a broken hand," Ty replied. "I'll be overseeing the swimming and doing any chores I can manage. Just call me Ty Sullivan, *handyman*," he added sarcastically.

Kenny suddenly remembered what Melly had said yesterday. That this guy wasn't Ty. So who was he?

"I was talking to some friends yesterday," Kenny said. "They told me they thought you were somebody else. Somebody with another name."

"Well . . . I'm also known as *Superman*," Ty

growled. "What is this—an interrogation?" Then he reached into his back pocket and pulled out his wallet. He slapped it on the desk and opened it up.

Kenny peered through the clear plastic at the driver's license. Ty's face gazed back at him, looking like a mug shot. Kenny read the name— Tyler Sullivan.

Kenny stared at it, confused. Why did Melly say he wasn't Ty? he wondered. She sounded so positive.

"Hey." Ty's voice broke into Kenny's thoughts. "Stay out of my face from now on," he warned. He spoke softly, but Kenny could hear the anger in his voice.

Ty's fist shot out. Kenny flinched, expecting to feel the knuckles slam into his face.

Laughing coldly, Ty picked up his wallet and stuffed it into his pocket. "Scared you, didn't I?" he asked. "That's good. If you're scared, you'll be careful. But if you're not . . ." Ty pointed at Kenny, his thumb and forefinger like a gun.

Kenny shouldered him aside and left the office without speaking. He didn't know what Ty's problem was. But he knew one thing for sure—the guy was definitely dangerous.

In the big clearing Kenny rounded up his group. Graydon and Charlie were back to shoving each other again. Dan, David, Matthew, and

Simon chatted together. Every once in a while one of them would glance sideways at Vincent, then whisper something to the others.

Kenny knew they were wondering what Vincent's face looked like. Kenny wondered the same thing. It must be really gross, he thought.

Vincent had to know the others were talking about him, but he just kept staring straight ahead through the eyeholes of his ski mask.

When Kenny approached, Vincent immediately ran over and stood by him.

Kenny forced himself to pat the kid on the shoulder. "Hey, Vincent, how's it going?"

"Okay," Vincent murmured. He edged even closer to Kenny, gazing at him intently.

Kenny felt uneasy as those blue eyes focused on him. Why does he keep staring at me? What is he thinking? What does he want?

He felt like telling the kid to scram. Or at least act normal.

But he's *not* normal, he reminded himself. He patted Vincent's shoulder again. "Okay, guys, everybody up for arts-and-crafts?" he asked.

Charlie made a gagging sound. "Not me. I hate that baby stuff."

"Too bad." Kenny began herding them along the path. *He* was ready for arts-and-crafts. After all, Melly would be there.

His heart began to pound in anticipation.

Inside the arts-and-crafts cabin stood long

tables and benches, boxes of rocks and
pinecones, paints, construction paper, and other
supplies. A soft breeze blew through the window,
stirring a mobile of balsa-wood ducks that hung
from the ceiling.

The place was empty.

"I guess the counselor isn't here yet," Kenny
said. He started for the door.

Vincent grabbed his arm. "Where are you
going?"

"To try to find the counselor." Kenny took
another step, but Vincent clung to his arm.

"You can't go," he declared. "You're supposed
to stay with us all the time!"

One of the other boys snickered.

Vincent dug his fingers into Kenny's arm. "I'm
coming with you!"

No way, Kenny thought. He didn't want Vincent
clinging to him like a leech every second. He
couldn't help it—the kid made his skin crawl.

"No, you stay here," Kenny told him. "I'll be
right back. Really."

Vincent's eyes narrowed. He let go of Kenny's
arm and stalked to the other side of the cabin.

"I'll be right back," Kenny repeated. "Nobody
leave." He hurried outside and glanced around.

"Kenny, how are you feeling?" Dana asked as
she and her group headed toward the lake.

"Fine. Great." Now that I'm away from Vincent,
he thought.

"By the way, I saw Melly when I first got here," Dana told him. "Have you talked to her yet?"

Kenny shook his head. "Do you know where she is now?"

"No. But if I see her, I'll tell her you're looking for her. I'm sure she'd want to know." Dana smiled sweetly. "Jade would too."

"Knock it off," Kenny snapped. "My group's supposed to have arts-and-crafts, and she's not here."

"Like I said, I'll tell her," Dana repeated as she walked on.

Kenny frowned after her. Is she kidding me? he wondered. He couldn't be sure. But he'd worry about it later. Right now he wanted to find Melly. Ty and Dana both saw her earlier—so where was she?

Kenny decided to check the office building. Maybe she had to make a phone call or something. He glanced back at the cabin. The kids will be all right, he thought. As he started down the trail, a piercing scream rang out.

A shrill scream of pain—from the arts-and-crafts cabin.

Kenny's heart stuttered, then began to race. Spinning around, he tore back up the trail and burst into the cabin.

And saw Vincent.

On the floor, groaning and writhing in pain.

Covered in blood.

Chapter Eight

"**W**hat happened?" Kenny cried. He dived across the room and dropped onto his knees next to Vincent. The boy lay still now, his eyes closed beneath the wool mask.

Kenny was afraid to touch him. "What happened?" he repeated, gazing up at the other boys.

"We didn't see anything," Dan replied in a high, frightened voice. "We were checking out the stuff in the boxes. Then he screamed. When we turned around, he was lying on the floor."

"Is he dead?" Simon asked.

"No, jerk. Can't you see he's breathing?" Graydon declared.

Graydon is right, Kenny thought. The kid is

breathing, at least. He bent close to the masked face.

Wait a sec . . . what was that smell?

Kenny swabbed his finger in the red stuff on Vincent's arm and sniffed it.

Paint!

Kenny felt a surge of anger. How many times was Vincent going to do this to them?

He grabbed the boy by the front of the shirt— and jerked him to a sitting position.

"Enough!" he screamed. "Enough of these stupid jokes!"

Without even realizing it, he was shaking Vincent hard.

Vincent's eyes snapped open in fear. Beneath the mask the boy's mouth opened in a whimper.

Kenny caught the other boys' disapproving stares. He let go of Vincent's shirt and swallowed hard. "Sorry," he murmured. "I didn't mean to lose it. But you've got to stop scaring everyone, Vincent. It isn't funny."

Vincent glared at Kenny through the eyeholes in the mask. "You shouldn't have left me," he declared.

Whoa. Was that it? Kenny wondered. Vincent was getting revenge because I wouldn't let him come with me? This kid is really twisted.

Kenny forced himself to sound calm. "Go to the cabin and get cleaned up," he told Vincent. "Then come right back here."

Vincent climbed to his feet slowly, adjusting his mask. Then he stomped out the door.

Kenny let out a long sigh. I know the kid is troubled, he thought. But I really can't stand him.

Melly arrived while the boys were wiping the floor. Kenny felt his heart lift. She really *is* okay, he thought with relief.

"What happened with Vincent?" she asked. "I saw him out on the path. How did he get all that paint on himself?"

"He decided to take a bath in it," Kenny replied bitterly.

"Huh?"

"Never mind." Kenny reached out and tucked a strand of silky blond hair behind her ear. "I was so worried last night, Melly. I mean, where did you go? I thought you drowned!"

Melly's face flushed. "I'm so sorry. I . . . I never thought you'd really jump," she stammered. "When I saw you go under and your friends started screaming, I . . . I ran for help."

"I searched for you," Kenny said. "I—"

"By the time I got back, you were gone," Melly continued. "I felt so bad. I mean, I was the one who made you jump. I'm really sorry, Kenny."

"Hey, don't worry about it," he replied. "I'm just glad you're okay."

Melly raised her hand and gently touched the small cut on Kenny's right temple. "I'm glad *you* are," she murmured.

"Oh, yuck, are you guys gonna start smooching?" Graydon complained.

Charlie made a choking sound.

Kenny laughed. "I guess I'll go and let you do your arts-and-crafts thing," he told Melly. "Can I see you later? After the buses leave? Maybe we could take a walk in the woods."

"Definitely. I'll meet you on the nature trail, okay?" Melly kissed him quickly on the cheek. "And I can't wait."

When the last of the buses pulled out later that afternoon, Kenny finger-combed his hair and brushed the dust from his shorts.

Time to meet Melly, he thought eagerly, hurrying along the path toward the nature trail. He'd thought of her all day, through swimming and lunch and softball and hiking.

He'd thought of Jade, too. Pictured her sitting in a stuffy classroom, taking that SAT prep course. Probably thinking about him.

I'm cheating on her, he told himself. It's not fair. And it's not fair to Melly, either. I should tell her about Jade.

But what if Melly decides not to see me anymore?

Kenny walked past the office building, then changed his mind and went inside. Craig's office was empty. Kenny quickly scanned the list of counselors on the bulletin board. He found Melly's phone number and address in Waynesbridge and scribbled it on a piece of camp notepaper.

I'll surprise her one of these nights, he thought. He trotted outside and hurried to the nature trail. I'll show up at her house and take her out to a movie or something. And then we'll take a long drive and park. And then . . .

"What are you hanging around here for?" a girl's voice said from behind him.

Kenny spun around, startled.

Dana and Debra stood with their duffel bags slung over their shoulders. "Camp's over for the day, remember?" Dana asked. "Aren't you going home?"

"In a few minutes," Kenny replied.

Dana gave him a suspicious look. "What are you waiting for?"

Before Kenny could think of an excuse, he spotted Melly walking toward them.

Following Kenny's gaze, Dana glanced over her shoulder.

"Come on, Dana!" Debra urged. "I want to get to the mall."

"Go ahead," Dana told her. "I'll be there in just a second."

As Debra hurried off, Dana turned back to Kenny. "I was just joking about you and Melly before," she declared. "Now I see it wasn't a joke. Jade's your girlfriend, Kenny. If you don't have the guts to tell her about Melly, then I will."

Dana didn't give him a chance to reply. She turned and ran after Debra, passing Melly without a word.

Kenny felt shaken by Dana's threat. Would she really tell Jade? Or did she just enjoy having something to hold over his head?

I can't be sure, he thought. But I don't want to stop seeing Melly. I just have to be more careful from now on.

"What's wrong?" Melly asked as she joined him. She wrapped her arms around his neck and kissed him. "You look worried."

I *can't* tell her about Jade, Kenny thought.

"What is it?" Melly whispered. "Tell me."

Kenny said the first thing that popped into his mind. "Ty. The guy really has it in for me."

Melly drew back. "What do you mean?"

"He thinks I'm out to get him or something," Kenny replied. "He accused me of breaking his hand on purpose. And then, when you told me his name isn't Ty—"

"It isn't," Melly interrupted. "It can't be."

"Well, that's the name on his driver's license," Kenny told her. "I saw it."

Melly stared at him, confused.

"Anyway," Kenny continued, "I asked him about it, and that's when he threatened me."

Melly's jaw tightened. "I warned you," she muttered. "If Tyler threatened you, he definitely meant it. He's vicious. Evil."

Kenny frowned. She's so intense, he thought. She shouldn't be *this* upset. "Hey, relax," he said, pulling her close.

Melly stood stiffly for a few seconds. Then her attitude shifted again. She leaned against him and kissed his neck. "Don't worry about Ty anymore," she murmured softly. She kissed his lips.

As Kenny kissed her back, he forgot about Jade and Dana and Ty. Nothing matters when I'm with Melly, he thought.

Melly stepped back and took his hand. "Come on, let's go into the woods. It's much cooler in there."

Kenny gave her hand a squeeze, and they began walking.

Pine trees blocked out most of the sun. A squirrel fussed at them from its perch on one of the trunks. But that was the only noise. Weird. No birds, Kenny thought. I never noticed that before.

"It's so beautiful in here," Melly murmured.

Kenny stopped walking and tried to kiss her. But Melly pulled away.

"See that cave?" she asked, pointing.

Kenny glanced toward the opening on the other side of the trail. "Sure. That's where we had Vincent's phony bat attack."

"Well, there aren't any bats, but it *is* a dangerous place," Melly told him. "It's haunted."

Kenny gave her a skeptical glance. "Come on."

"It is," she insisted. "Nobody talks about it, of course. But a little boy got lost in that cave one summer. He died in there. They buried his body, but his spirit lives on—in that cave."

Kenny stared at her. *Does she really believe that story?*

"Come on, let's go see if the spirit is in there now!" Melly cried. Dropping Kenny's hand, she darted across the trail and disappeared into the dark mouth of the cave.

"Melly, wait up!" Kenny hurried after her. He plunged into the cave and immediately stumbled on some rocks. "Melly?" he shouted, waving his arms for balance.

"Up ahead!" she called. Then she laughed. An evil, haunted-house-type laugh. The sound echoed through the darkness. "Follow me!"

"I can't even see you!" Kenny moved cautiously ahead. The walls of the cave narrowed and twisted to the left. Kenny glanced back at the opening, where he could still see daylight.

"Come on, Kenny!" Melly urged. Her echoing voice sounded fainter this time. Farther away.

The walls closed in even more. The ceiling grew lower. A sour odor filled the air. Kenny walked hunched over, following the sound of Melly's evil laugh as it bounced off the walls.

He couldn't see a thing.

"See any ghosts yet?" he called out.

No reply.

"Melly?" he shouted. "Melly!"

All he heard was the echo of his own voice.

The air grew cooler. A drop of cold water fell on Kenny's head and trickled down his neck. Something soft brushed against his face. A spiderweb?

A ghost?

Kenny shivered. Get a grip, he told himself.

"Melly?" he called again.

No reply.

The passage twisted again. Then it widened until Kenny could stretch his arms out and not feel the walls anymore. He stood up straight.

"Melly!" he shouted.

"Melly . . . Melly . . . Melly!" echoed back.

Kenny took another step.

And felt nothing under his foot.

"No!" he cried. He flailed his arms and tried to catch himself.

Too late.

Too late.

He tumbled off the edge and fell . . . fell through endless darkness.

Chapter Nine

"**Y**AAII!"

Kenny landed hard on both feet.

He heard his knees crack. Pain shot up his legs.

He toppled forward. Onto the hard, rocky ground. He rolled to his side and clutched his knee, sucking air between his teeth.

"Melly!" he choked out. What happened to her? Had she fallen too? Was she lying here in the dark with a broken neck? "Melly!"

A light appeared. A small flame, flickering in the darkness.

Gasping in pain and fear, Kenny peered up at it.

Melly gazed down from above him, holding a lighter. The flame lit her face from below, turning her chin and cheeks bloodred.

Kenny caught his breath. "Where *were* you?" he demanded. "Didn't you hear me calling you?"

A strange smile played over her face. "Don't you like to play hide-and-seek?"

Kenny didn't answer. He rose to his feet, rubbing his knee and staring around. He'd landed in some kind of crater, strewn with jagged pebbles and chunks of rock. Melly stood high above him, gazing down from a rocky ledge.

That's what I fell from, he thought, feeling a surge of anger. I'm lucky I didn't break my neck. He took a step and winced as the weight hit his sore knee. "Why didn't you warn me about this hole?" he asked.

The light went out. Melly gave her eerie laugh and flicked it on again, holding it to the side. "I told you this was a dangerous place."

Kenny stared up at her. Shadows hid most of her face, but he could see the teasing sparkle in her eyes. "I suppose the ghost made me fall, huh?"

"Did you see the ghost?" she asked, her expression turning serious.

"I don't believe in ghosts," he told her.

"You should," she replied. She dropped to her knees and stretched her arm down toward him. "Come on, I'll give you a hand up."

Kenny limped over and grasped her hand. He felt a shiver of excitement as they touched, and his anger drained away.

She's acting so weird. I should be furious with her, but it's impossible, he thought. I'm crazy about her.

The lighter went out. With Melly's help, Kenny climbed up the crater's rocky side and swung onto the ledge. He stood up slowly, testing his knee.

"Better now?" Melly asked.

"It's fine." Kenny shivered in the cool, damp air. "Let's get out of here," he said, slipping an arm around her shoulders.

"But it's so nice like this." Melly snuggled close. She pressed her forehead against his cheek. Then she kissed him. "Let's stay just a little while longer."

Kenny desperately wanted to leave. "We can be alone in the woods, you know."

"It's not the same," she protested, sliding her lips down the side of his face. "I like being with you, all alone in the dark. Well, almost alone," she added.

Kenny pulled back. "What do you mean? Who's here?"

Melly brushed her lips against his ear. "The spirit," she murmured softly.

Kenny smoothed the soft blond hair back from her face and gazed into her eyes. "But . . ."

"But what?" Melly asked.

"Ssh!" Kenny told her. He'd heard something. He was sure of it.

"What's going on?" Melly whispered. "Do you hear the ghost?"

"Just wait." Kenny stood still, listening. He heard his heartbeat pulsing in his ears. Water dripping from the roof of the cave.

Then he heard the sound again. A soft *whoosh*. Steady. Rhythmic.

The sound of breathing.

Not his. Not Melly's.

Kenny's scalp prickled. His heart pounded harder. Someone's in here! he thought.

Someone *is* watching us.

"Let me have the lighter," Kenny whispered.

"Why? What's wrong?"

"I don't know yet." Kenny's heart raced. "Just give me the lighter!"

Melly slipped Kenny the plastic lighter. He spun around, flicked it on, and held it high.

A ghostly pale face peered at them from around the bend in the tunnel.

Kenny gasped. "I don't believe it!"

Chapter Ten

A stocky figure in shorts and a dirt-smeared T-shirt leaped into the open. "Ha!" Graydon shouted. "Gotcha!"

Kenny took a deep breath and waited for his heart to slow down. "What are you doing here?" he demanded.

"Watching you," Graydon replied, grinning.

Kenny scowled at him. "Your bus left twenty minutes ago. Why weren't you on it?"

"The stupid bus left without me," Graydon said. "I started to go to the office, but then I saw you two sneaking into the woods."

"And you decided to follow us?" Kenny asked.

Graydon shrugged. "Why not?"

"Because your parents are probably freaking out about now, wondering where you are," Kenny replied. "And you could have gotten hurt in this cave. And it's not very cool to follow people and sneak up on them."

"Whatever." Graydon shrugged again.

Kenny rolled his eyes and turned to Melly. "I need to walk him back and call his house," he told her.

"I understand." Melly shot Graydon an annoyed glance. "I'll see you tomorrow, Kenny." She brushed her fingers against his arm, making his skin tingle. Then she hurried through the cave ahead of them.

Graydon snickered. "Ooh, is your girlfriend mad?"

"She's not my girlfriend." Or is she? Kenny wondered. An image of Jade popped into his mind, but he quickly pushed it out. He didn't want to think about Jade right now.

Gripping his hands over Graydon's shoulders, he turned him around and marched him down the passageway.

By the time they emerged from the cave, Melly had disappeared.

"Tomorrow is the overnight, isn't it?" Graydon asked. He bent over to pick up a twig as they started back to the camp.

Kenny nodded. The camp had overnights once a week. Tomorrow would be the first. "Don't forget to bring your sleeping bag."

"I won't. It'll be fun. Except for the weirdo," Graydon added.

Kenny glanced at him. "You mean Vincent."

"Who else?" Graydon flipped the twig up and caught it. "What a freak."

Kenny kept quiet, even though he felt he should argue with Graydon.

"I bet his face is really disgusting," Graydon said.

"Hey, you think he'll ever let us see it?"

"Probably not," Kenny replied. "Listen, I know the mask looks weird, but don't make fun of him. Try to be nice to him."

"Why should I? He's a jerk." Graydon snapped the twig in two and tossed the pieces into the trees. Then he raced down the trail, leaving Kenny behind.

Kenny shook his head. Everybody said nine-year-olds would be fun, he thought. Easy to handle.

Yeah, right.

When Kenny reached the office, Craig told him that Graydon's mother had already come to get him. "What happened?" Craig asked. "How did he get left behind?"

"I'm not sure. He said he missed the bus, so he took a walk in the woods." Kenny decided not to mention the cave.

Craig started to say something, but the phone rang. He picked it up and gave Kenny a good-bye wave. As Kenny stepped into the hall, he spotted

Ty standing near the front door. Ty was staring at several cans of white paint stacked against the wall.

Be cool, Kenny told himself. Maybe the guy finally realized I didn't mean to break his hand. "Hey, Ty. What's the paint for?"

Ty turned and narrowed his eyes at the sight of Kenny. "I have to paint some of the cabins."

Kenny frowned. "With one hand?"

"Yeah, it's going to be lots of fun," Ty replied sarcastically.

Kenny stuck his hands in his pockets. "Listen, I'm really sorry. I—"

"Don't waste your breath," Ty snapped.

Kenny gritted his teeth and reached for the door handle.

"Going to meet your girlfriend?" Ty asked. "You must like living dangerously."

Kenny frowned. "What's that supposed to mean?"

"It means Melly's a nut case. I told you she keeps giving me the evil eye," Ty reminded him.

Yeah, because you're a jerk, Kenny thought.

"But I ran into her a few minutes ago," Ty continued. "And this time she did more than just stare at me."

"Like what?"

"Like this." Ty stuck his arm out. Two long scratches ran up his forearm. Blood still oozed over the ragged edges of skin.

"Huh? Melly did that?" Kenny gasped.

Ty nodded. "She's crazy, man. I'm warning you. She's out of control."

"But—" Kenny stared at the deep scratches down Ty's arm.

"She's evil," Ty murmured. "I'm not kidding. She's evil." He narrowed his eyes at Kenny. "Do you believe me?"

Chapter Eleven

"**T**hey hear a rustling noise outside the car." Kenny lowered his voice to a fearful whisper. "It's coming closer . . . closer."

Kenny's group huddled around the campfire, frozen in silence as they listened to him tell a ghost story.

"The girl turns her head." Kenny paused, then finished in a shout. "And *the severed hand* grabs her by the throat!"

The boys jumped, gasping.

Kenny laughed, then reached for a marshmallow and poked it onto a stick. He held it over the flames and glanced around.

Several more fires dotted the campground, with kids and their counselors sitting around them. Some of them sang songs, others were telling stories. Kenny spotted Dana across the field, teaching her campers a cheerleading routine.

He brought his gaze back to his group. All of the guys seemed to be having a good time. Except for Vincent.

Vincent sat apart. He would have sat next to Kenny, but Kenny had made sure there wasn't room. He felt a little guilty. But Kenny couldn't help it. He didn't want Vincent clinging to him all the time—it was too creepy.

Vincent obviously wasn't happy. He glared at Kenny, his eyes mirroring the flames of the campfire.

Kenny glanced away, shivering in spite of the fire's heat. Every time he looked at Vincent, the kid was watching him. It was eerie, threatening. And even though Vincent had never done anything, Kenny felt edgy all the time, as if he were being stalked.

And now he's mad at me, Kenny said to himself, his stomach churning. I'll never admit it out loud, but the kid kind of scares me. It's so embarrassing.

"Hey, tell another story," Matthew said, interrupting Kenny's thoughts. "And make it scarier. I've heard the hand one before."

"Oh, sure. So how come you practically had a cow at the end?" Charlie asked.

Vincent unfolded his skinny legs and stood up.

"I have to go to the bathroom," he murmured.

"Sure," Kenny told him. "Go ahead."

Vincent adjusted the red-and-white ski mask. Then he left the campfire and headed down the trail toward the latrine.

Charlie elbowed Matthew. He pointed to Vincent. They both snickered.

"Cut it out," Kenny told them. He felt he had to stick up for Vincent in front of the other campers. But he also felt glad the kid had left. He ate the marshmallow and tossed the stick into the fire. "I'm going to walk around for a minute," he told the group. "You guys stay here."

"I thought you were going to tell more stories," David said.

"Why don't *you* tell one?" Kenny suggested as he stood up and glanced across the camp. Good, he thought. Craig's not around. I can stretch my legs and not get reamed for leaving my group for a second. He strolled over to Debra's campfire. Her six-year-olds weren't on the overnight, but she had volunteered to help with another group. "Are we having fun yet?" he asked her.

"I'd rather be out with Clark," she whispered. "I bet you'd rather be with Jade, too."

Kenny nodded. He stared at her for a second, trying to decide if she was being sarcastic. But Debra seemed totally sincere. Good. At least Dana hadn't told Debra about Melly. Maybe she wouldn't tell Jade.

Kenny walked around for a few more minutes, then started back toward his group. As he passed a small grove of trees on the edge of the campground, someone grabbed his shoulder from behind.

"Whoa!" Kenny jumped and spun around. "Melly!"

"Hi." Melly stood on tiptoe and kissed him. "Did I scare you?"

"Uh . . . yeah, a little." Kenny quickly glanced around. Had Dana spotted them? No, she was leading her group in another cheer, her back to them.

Melly squeezed his arm. As Kenny felt her nails on his skin, he glanced down, remembering Ty's story.

"What's the matter?" Melly asked, following his gaze.

"Nothing. I just . . ." Kenny hesitated for a second. "Listen, this is probably crazy, but Ty told me you . . . you attacked him yesterday."

Melly's fingers tightened. Kenny winced as her nails dug in harder. Her breathing grew fast and her eyes flashed.

Then the moment was over. Melly loosened her fingers and stroked Kenny's arm. "I did scratch Ty," she admitted. "I bumped into him, and he started yelling at me. Then he grabbed me. I had to scratch him to get away. I told you he was dangerous."

Kenny stared at her. Her fingertips brushed his skin, feeling warm and silky now. A campfire flickered in her eyes and turned her hair a reddish-gold.

Kenny's throat went dry. Ty is the crazy one, he realized. Not Melly.

Melly is fantastic.

Melly leaned close and whispered, "Meet me here after lights out." She squeezed his hand and left, picking her way through the campfires.

As Kenny started back to his group, he glanced across the campground again—and felt a jolt of panic. Dana was facing his way now. Had she seen him with Melly?

Kenny waved to her, trying to look casual. Dana waved back. Good, he thought. If she had seen us, she'd come over and chew me out.

Kenny turned back toward his group and spotted Vincent approaching the campfire. The boy stood awkwardly, glancing around.

He's looking for me, Kenny thought with a shudder. I wish I didn't have to go back.

With a sigh, Kenny reluctantly strolled over to the fire.

"You missed David's ghost story," Dan told him. "It was awesome."

"I liked the severed-hand one better," Simon declared. He twisted his hand into a claw and thrust it at Graydon's face.

Graydon batted it away and jumped up.

Holding his arms out, he staggered stiffly around the fire, like Frankenstein's monster.

The others quickly leaped to their feet, grunting and grabbing each other by the throat.

Kenny glanced at Vincent. He stood to the side, watching Kenny through his mask. Not blinking . . . Not blinking.

Kenny sat down near the fire and took another marshmallow from the plastic bag. He reached for a new stick—then stopped, his hand suspended in the air. "Hey, guys." His voice came out weak and shaky. He swallowed and tried again. "Hey. Everybody stop and stay exactly where you are!"

The boys shuffled to a stop. "Why?" Graydon whined.

Kenny pointed to the pile of sticks. As he did, one of them moved.

A snake.

Slowly the snake inched toward the warmth of the fire. Its thick, greenish-brown body rippled in the dirt. Its wedge-shaped head swayed back and forth.

"Whoa!" Charlie gasped. He took a step backwards.

The snake lifted its head. Its tongue darted out, probing the air.

"Don't move!" Kenny whispered hoarsely. "It's poisonous."

The boys froze.

"Are you sure?" Simon whispered, barely moving his lips. "Are you sure it's poisonous?"

"Yes," Kenny replied, not taking his eyes off the snake. "I learned it when I was a Boy Scout. This one's really dangerous."

The snake slithered a little closer to the fire, then stopped again. Its tongue flicked out.

"Do something!" David urged.

Kenny's heart raced. We can't just run, he told himself. Someone would get bitten.

Kenny's mouth felt like cotton. He licked his lips. "Just stay still," he whispered.

Kenny took a breath. He raised his arm and slowly stretched his hand toward the snake.

The snake lifted its head higher.

The blood roared in Kenny's ears. Slow and easy, he told himself. Don't jerk your arm. Just one smooth movement. Grab it right behind the head.

Now!

Chapter Twelve

Kenny shot his hand out.

The snake whipped around. Its jaws snapped open. Its head darted like an arrow toward Kenny's hand.

"Oh, no!" Kenny let out a shriek. He stumbled back.

Did it bite me? Did it?

He stared at his hand. Smooth. No puncture holes.

He stared down at the snake. It prepared to strike again.

And he hadn't felt a sting, he realized.

"Okay, everybody hold still," Kenny choked out. "One, two, three!"

Kenny took a deep breath. Tensed his muscles. And grabbed the snake behind the head. The

73

snake writhed and struggled. But Kenny clamped his fingers tight.

"What are you going to do with it?" Dan asked as Kenny jumped to his feet. "Chop it in half?"

"No, I'll take it to the rec hall," Kenny replied breathlessly. "They keep some cages there in case somebody finds a wounded bird or something. I'll put it in one of them. You guys stay here."

Holding the wriggling snake at arm's length, Kenny quick-stepped along the path until he came to the empty rec hall. Three of the cages had bars. No good. The fourth was made of strong wire mesh. Kenny lifted the lid, dropped the snake inside, and slammed the lid shut.

The snake writhed furiously, slamming its head against the metal and darting its tongue in and out.

Craig will get rid of it tomorrow, Kenny thought as he hurried back to the campfire. Let's hope he takes it really far away.

Even before he reached the campfire, Kenny heard Graydon. "Snap!" the kid was shouting. "Snap-snap! I got you! The poison is spreading! When it reaches your heart, you die!"

In the firelight Kenny saw Graydon pretending to be a snake. "Snap!" he cried, baring his teeth at Vincent.

Vincent stepped back.

Graydon circled him. "Ssss!" he hissed. "I'll get

you. I'll sink my fangs into you. You will die a slow, painful death! Sssssnap!"

As Graydon lunged, Vincent jumped back, his eyes wide.

"Hey, guys, calm down before somebody falls in the fire," Kenny called out.

"Sssnap!" Graydon cried, pinching Vincent's arm.

"Come on, guys, cool it," Kenny said.

"I'm not doing anything!" Vincent cried. He pointed at Graydon. "*He* is! Tell *him* to stop!"

Graydon thumped to the ground and crossed his legs. "What a baby," he muttered under his breath.

"Don't call me that!" Vincent shouted. He glared at Kenny. "Tell him, Kenny! Tell him not to call me names!"

I can't believe this, Kenny thought. The kid is flipping out. "No names, Graydon," he said.

"Is that it?" Vincent demanded. "That's all you're going to say?"

Kenny motioned for the others to sit down. Then he pulled Vincent aside and patted him on the shoulder. "Relax, okay? It's over."

Vincent shrugged his hand off. "You didn't stick up for me," he murmured in a cold voice. "I won't forget it."

A shiver ran up Kenny's spine. Was that some kind of threat?

"Hey, Kenny!" Graydon called. "Come on, let's do something."

"Good idea." Kenny pulled Vincent back to the circle of kids. "How about playing a game, like twenty questions?"

"Boring," Charlie moaned. "Let's tell more ghost stories."

"I have something *much* scarier than ghost stories," Vincent announced. He reached into his pocket and pulled out a deck of cards held together by a grimy rubber band.

"Cards?" Dan rolled his eyes. "Are you kidding?"

"They're not regular cards. These are Doom Teller cards. They predict the future," Vincent told them. "And they're always right."

Kenny tried to laugh, but the solemn look in Vincent's eyes gave him a chill.

"Where'd you get 'em?" Graydon asked with a sneer. "In a cereal box? Are those Barney cards?"

Everyone laughed.

Vincent waited for the laughter to stop. "My grandfather gave them to me."

"So how do you play?" Graydon asked. "Do you bet money?"

Vincent ignored the question. He fanned the deck out. "You pick three cards," he said. "But you can't look at them. Just put them facedown on the ground."

He turned to Kenny. "Why don't you go first, Kenny? They'll tell your future."

Kenny felt the chill again, but he tried to shrug

it off. Don't be a wimp, he told himself. It's just a game.

"Pick three cards," Vincent repeated.

Kenny took three cards and placed them in a row in the dirt.

Vincent set the rest of the pack down and picked up the first card Kenny had chosen. He stared at it, then at Kenny, his eyes cold and unblinking behind the mask.

The skin prickled on the back of Kenny's neck. "What?" he asked.

Vincent shook his head. He picked up the second card and peered down at it. His breathing grew faster. His skinny fingers tightened on the cards.

"Vincent." Kenny tried to keep his voice calm, but he could feel Vincent's fear inside himself. "What do you see?"

Vincent didn't reply. Slowly he reached out and picked up the third card. When he stared up at Kenny, his eyes bulged with fear.

Kenny's heart thudded and his palms grew sweaty. "What is it?" he demanded. "Tell me!"

Vincent set the cards faceup in the dirt.

As Kenny stared at them, his terror grew stronger. His heart raced.

Each card had a skull on it. A black skull, with empty, sunken eye sockets and teeth bared in a hideous grin.

"Three black skulls." Vincent's shrill voice

shook with fear. "That's so horrible! I've never seen that."

"What does that mean?" Kenny demanded, staring at the masked boy. "What?"

A tiny smirk formed on Vincent's lips.

"Instant death," he replied.

Chapter Thirteen

Another shiver of fear ran up Kenny's spine as he gazed down at the black skulls.

The glow from the campfire turned the skulls' bony cheeks crimson, and the flames seemed to flicker in their empty eyes.

"Instant death—ha!" Dan scoffed. "So how come Kenny's still breathing, Vincent?"

"It doesn't have to happen this very second," Vincent declared.

"Oh, yeah? News flash, Vinnie—that's what *instant* means." Graydon snatched up the cards and tossed them into the air. "Anyway, I have a better game—fifty-two pickup!" He reached for the rest of the deck.

"Hey!" Vincent cried. "Leave them alone!" He grabbed the deck and held it tight as Graydon tried to pry his fingers loose.

"Cut it out!" Vincent shouted. He toppled onto his side, and Graydon fell on top of him. "Get off me!"

Graydon laughed. "First give me the stupid cards!"

"Okay, enough!" Kenny called out.

"Get off me!" Vincent shouted again as he and Graydon rolled over in the dirt. Vincent kicked out with his foot, hitting the edge of the campfire.

A burning twig skittered across the dirt, sending a shower of sparks into the air. The rest of the boys jumped back.

"Break it up!" Kenny demanded. He kicked the twig back into the fire, grabbed both boys by an arm, and hauled them to their feet. "You want to get burned?"

Vincent's eyes flashed as he stared up at Kenny.

Kenny quickly dropped his arm.

Vincent shoved the deck into his pocket and straightened his ski mask.

Graydon shot him a dirty look. "It was *his* fault," he declared, pointing at Vincent. "He kicked the stick out of the fire. All I wanted to do was look at the cards."

"Try asking next time," Kenny suggested.

"Yeah, yeah." Graydon scuffed some dirt into the fire.

"Good idea," Kenny told him. "Time to put the fire out and bunk down for the night."

As the boys began to smother the fire with dirt, Kenny reached for the empty marshmallow bag. He spotted the three black skull cards Graydon had tossed in the air. All three had landed faceup.

Kenny shuddered as he stared at their empty eyes and evil death-grins. I've already had three close calls, he thought. Jumping off the rock, falling in the cave, the poisonous snake . . .

It's a game, he told himself. Just a card game.

"I had to call you," Jade declared over the phone later that night. "I hope you weren't asleep."

"Are you kidding? I'm wide awake." Kenny stood in Craig's office, holding the phone with a shaking hand. His group had finally gone to sleep when another counselor told him he had an emergency phone call. "Are you okay?" he asked Jade. "What's the emergency?"

"I didn't say it was an emergency," Jade replied. "I said it was urgent. And it is—I miss you."

Kenny sank down into Craig's chair and puffed out a breath. "You had me scared!"

"I'm sorry. As I said, I miss you," Jade told him. "Hey, if you were scared, that means you *care* about me, right?"

"Sure I do." Remembering he was supposed to meet Melly later, Kenny felt his cheeks get hot.

It's a good thing Jade can't see me, he thought. She'd know something is wrong. "How's the SAT course?" he asked.

"Awful. Boring. Harder than I thought it would be." She laughed. "But the ocean's great. How's camp?"

"Harder than I thought it would be." Propping a foot on Craig's desk, Kenny began to tell her about camp and his group of boys. Jade laughed at his jokes. She sympathized when he told her about Ty and sounded concerned when he described how strange Vincent was. He even told her that the kid scared him a little. And Jade didn't laugh.

As he talked, Kenny suddenly realized how glad he was to be talking to her.

I *do* miss her, he told himself.

He felt a rush of guilt as he thought of Melly again. Melly is different, he thought. She's strange and exciting. I don't know what happened, but I guess I went kind of crazy for a while. It's like Melly put a spell on me or something.

But Jade is my girlfriend. I can't cheat on her. I don't want to cheat on her.

I have to tell Melly about Jade, he decided. I have to call it off between us. Tonight.

Melly stood in the open clearing, staring into the woods. In jeans and a navy-blue sweatshirt, she seemed to blend with the darkness. Only her pale hair stood out.

When she heard Kenny's footsteps, she turned. Her eyes lit up as she watched him walk toward her. "Hi," she murmured softly. "I knew you'd come."

"Yeah." Kenny stopped a couple of feet away from her and stuck his hands in his pockets. "I don't think we should stay out too late, though."

"Why not?" Melly moved closer. "Nobody knows. Anyway, wouldn't you like to take another walk with me?"

"Uh . . ."

Melly wrapped her arms around Kenny's neck and kissed him on the cheek. As she started to kiss his lips, he stepped back. "What's wrong?" she asked, dropping her arms.

"Nothing. I mean . . ." Kenny ran a hand through his hair. "Listen, I should have told you this before," he said. "I have a girlfriend."

Melly stared at him for a second. Then she laughed. "So what?"

"What do you mean?" Kenny asked. "I have a girlfriend. You're great, Melly. I really like you. A lot. But I don't want to get involved with anybody else right now."

She tossed her head and laughed again. "I don't believe you."

Kenny frowned at her, puzzled. "I thought you'd be angry," he told her. "Or unhappy."

"Sorry to disappoint you, but I'm not," she replied. "Do you want to know why? It's because I know you don't mean it. You don't want to break up with me. You just think you should."

Kenny shook his head. "Hey, listen . . . It's over, okay?"

"Well, I can change your mind, Kenny." Stepping close again, Melly gazed into his eyes. "I can. And I will."

Melly brushed her lips across his, then turned and strolled away toward one of the cabins.

Weird, Kenny thought as he walked back to his own cabin. What did she mean, she would change my mind? She sounded so sure. As if I don't have anything to say about it.

With a shrug he let himself into the cabin. I should have told her about Jade right up front, he decided. But Melly will get over it.

Inside the cabin Kenny paused, listening. All he heard was quiet, steady breathing. Good. The cabin stood dark, except for a thin stream of moonlight.

He waited for his eyes to adjust. Then he crept to his bed and sat down, leaning back against his rolled-up sleeping bag.

One of the boys mumbled something in his sleep.

Another one snorted as he turned over.

Kenny tugged his sweatshirt off and leaned back again.

And froze.

Something moved against his back.

Something alive.

Kenny forced himself to keep still. To wait.

A few seconds passed.

Kenny sat, barely breathing.

A few more seconds passed. He cautiously shifted his weight.

And froze in place. His heart thudded.

He felt it again. Something dry. Cold.

Slithering over his bare skin.

Chapter Fourteen

Kenny felt a rush of terror.

How big is the snake? he wondered. Is it poisonous?

He held himself rigid, afraid to let his breath out. Afraid to move.

The snake slithered slowly. Kenny could feel its scales scraping across his skin.

Don't panic, he told himself. Sit tight. Maybe it will crawl away.

The snake rubbed against Kenny's back. Kenny waited, biting his lips and listening to his heart pound.

This is torture, he thought. I have to do something. I can't just sit here or I'll go nuts.

Kenny turned his head as slowly as he could.

The snake stopped.

Kenny froze. Waited. Turned his head another inch. Glanced down out of the corner of his eye.

The snake raised its head. Its tongue flicked out. Half of its body was hidden behind Kenny, but the rest was clear. About an inch around, with brownish-green scales.

The same kind of snake as at the campfire, Kenny realized. Deadly poisonous.

The snake's head shot forward, jaws wide, fangs aimed at Kenny's bare skin.

Kenny leaped off the bed with a bellow of terror.

The shout woke the boys, who began screaming and scrambling around in their bunks.

"Don't get out of bed!" Kenny cried. He grabbed the snake and heaved it across the room. It hit the door and dropped to the floor with a thud.

The boys cried out in panic. Kenny wiped his forehead and swallowed. He was about to say something when he heard a muffled giggle.

Why would someone be laughing?

Out of fear? Or did one of them put the snake in my bed as some kind of sick joke?

Anger surged through him. He stalked to the center of the cabin, felt around for the light string, and yanked it on. The boys squinted and blinked as light flooded the room.

Kenny stared around.

Nobody was laughing now. The boys stared

back, sleepy-faced and rumpled. When they saw the snake, their eyes grew wide.

"Oh, wow!" Charlie exclaimed. "Was that in your bed?"

Kenny nodded. "It's stunned, for now."

Vincent shifted in his bunk. The boy's ski mask had ridden up a little. Kenny could see thick scars covering his neck like fat, red worms.

It must have been a horrible accident, Kenny thought with a shudder. No wonder he's disturbed.

Did Vincent do it? he wondered. He was furious with me because I didn't take his side against Graydon. He said he wouldn't forget it.

Is this his way of paying me back? Getting revenge? Is he sick enough to put that snake in my sleeping bag?

The snake quivered.

Kenny quickly grasped it behind the head, then pulled open the cabin door. "I'll be right back," he called out.

Hurrying through the night, Kenny raced to the rec hall. He made his way to the row of cages.

"Whoa!" he cried out as the cage where he'd put the snake came into view.

Empty.

The cage stood empty.

Kenny dropped the snake inside and shut the lid. This is the same snake, he realized. Someone took it out. Someone slipped it into my bed.

Someone crazy enough not to care if it bit me.

And Vincent's the only one like that. The only one who would do it.

Vincent.

I have to keep a closer eye on him.

A much closer eye.

The light was off when Kenny returned to the cabin.

Kenny yawned quietly, then tiptoed to his bed. Someone had unrolled his sleeping bag and put his pillow underneath. He reached down and flipped open the corner of the bag.

A weak shaft of moonlight fell across the white pillowcase. Kenny gazed down, shocked and frightened.

Three cards lay on top of the pillow.

Three cards with black skulls and empty eyes.

Chapter Fifteen

The smell of pancakes and syrup filled the dining hall the next morning. The campers gobbled their breakfast and told wild stories about a bear roaming the camp during the night.

"Come on—there was no bear," Charlie argued with the group at the next table.

"Yeah, but there *was* a snake—inside our cabin!" Graydon declared.

"A poisonous snake, right, Kenny?" Charlie asked.

"Right." Kenny drank some juice. He felt a chill as he remembered the feel of that snake, sliding against his skin.

He set the cup down and glanced at Vincent.

As usual, Vincent was watching him. But this

time Kenny didn't look away. I know what you did, he thought, staring into the boy's eyes. But why? Just because I didn't stick up for you the way you wanted? Do you really want to kill me? Are you *that* disturbed?

A whistle blew loudly, and Craig announced that breakfast was over. The campers scraped back their chairs, eager to get to their first activity. "Dump your trash first!" Kenny reminded them. Then he turned to Vincent and pulled him away from the table.

"Vincent, we need to talk," Kenny declared. He forced himself not to sound angry. The kid had problems. Serious problems. Yelling at him might totally send him over the edge. "I know you were mad at me last night," Kenny told him. "You thought I didn't stick up for you enough."

Vincent gazed at him, not speaking.

"It's okay to be mad," Kenny went on. "You can yell at me or ignore me or whatever."

Vincent kept quiet.

"But it's not okay to try to get revenge," Kenny told him. "I tried it once in grade school. I tripped a kid I was mad at—and the kid fell down the stairs and broke his arm. It could have been worse. I was out for revenge, and I did something dangerous. The snake last night—*that* was dangerous, too."

Vincent finally broke his silence. "I know," he said coldly. "You could be dead. You have to be careful."

*   *   *

I'm losing it, Kenny thought. I need to be by myself for a few minutes or I'll explode.

Eager to be alone, Kenny herded the boys to the archery range. He told one of the instructors he'd be back in ten minutes. Then he hurried off as if he had something urgent to take care of.

At the lakeside Kenny stopped running and gazed across the water. The shore stood empty for the moment. So quiet, Kenny thought, feeling grateful. He breathed deeply, then stretched out on his back and closed his eyes against the sun.

A couple of minutes passed. Kenny felt a shadow fall over his face. He opened his eyes and squinted up.

Melly stood over him.

So much for being alone, Kenny thought, sitting up. He gave her a wary glance.

"You look terrible," she declared. "Did your campers keep you awake all night or something?"

"You could say that." Kenny brushed some sand out of his hair as Melly dropped down next to him.

"So what's the problem?" Melly asked.

"This kid in my group," he replied. "He's really on my case."

"What do you mean? He talks back or something?"

Kenny shook his head. "No. I'm pretty sure he put a snake in my bed last night. It was poisonous—and he knew it."

Melly gasped.

"I tried to talk to him," Kenny said. "But I don't think I got through to him."

"How awful." Melly scooted closer. She slipped her hand in his and gave it a squeeze.

Kenny's shoulders stiffened.

Melly leaned closer and brushed her lips across his cheek.

"Hey, Melly . . ."

"Don't be so tense," she murmured, sliding her other hand along his neck. "Just relax and forget about everything. Everything but us."

"No way. Forget it." Kenny pulled free and jumped to his feet. "I thought maybe we could be friends, Melly. Just friends, okay? I already have a girlfriend—I told you that last night."

Melly rose to her feet. "And I told *you*—I'll make you change your mind."

She reached for him, but Kenny quickly stepped back. "Come on, Melly. Drop it, will you? This is embarrassing."

"You don't mean that," she insisted. "I know you don't. Admit it, Kenny!"

She really doesn't get the picture, Kenny thought.

"Admit it," Melly repeated. She closed the gap between them and wrapped her arms around his neck, trying to kiss him again.

Kenny pulled loose, angry now. "You want me

to spell it out?" he snapped. "Fine. Get lost, okay? You're not as hot as you think you are. *Now* do you get it?"

Melly gasped as if he'd punched her in the stomach. Her cheeks went white. Then they flamed with red, and her green eyes blazed. "You *do* care!" she shouted. "You *have* to!" She raised her hands to her face and raked her long, sharp nails down her cheeks. "You have to care, or I'll *die!*"

Kenny stared at the deep scratches in her cheeks. Blood began to seep between her fingers.

"I'll die if you leave me, do you hear?" Melly screamed, scratching her face again. "I can't live without you!"

Chapter Sixteen

"**I** can't live without you!" Melly screamed again, digging her nails into her skin. "Now do *you* get it?"

"Melly, stop it!" Kenny cried as the blood oozed down her cheeks. Horrified, he grabbed her wrists and yanked her hands away from her face.

Melly clutched his T-shirt, smearing it with blood. "Listen to me, Kenny!" Her voice rose even higher. "You can't leave me. I won't let you. I *can't* let you!"

Kenny tore her hands loose and stumbled backward.

Melly leaped for him.

Terrified by the wild gleam in her eyes, Kenny whirled around and began to run.

95

"Noooo!" Melly shrieked after him. "You can't leave me, Kenny! I'll die!"

Kenny picked up his pace, his heart pounding. Ty *was* right, he thought in horror. Melly is completely psycho.

As the last bus began to chug away from the camp, Kenny's shoulders sagged with relief. Talk about a bad day, he thought. This one was beyond belief.

"Kenny, are you okay?" Debra asked. She pointed to the reddish-brown streaks on the front of his shirt. "Did you cut yourself or something?"

"It's just ketchup," Kenny replied quickly. He'd been telling that to everyone who asked. No way he could explain that Melly had flipped out, scratching her face and smearing him with her blood.

"You want to come to Pete's Pizza?" Debra asked. "Dana and I are meeting Mickey there in about half an hour."

Kenny shook his head. He wanted to avoid Dana. "Thanks, but I just want to go home and veg out for a while."

And call Jade, he thought. Talking to her will make me forget everything else.

"Okay, see you tomorrow." Debra started toward the parking lot. "And change your shirt!" she called back over her shoulder. "It looks disgusting!"

Kenny waved and bent down to grab his duffel bag. As he straightened up, he spotted Ty Sullivan coming from the parking lot. The tall, blond counselor was swinging a can of paint in his good hand.

Kenny dropped to his knees and pretended to search for something in his bag. He definitely didn't need another run-in with Ty.

As Ty entered the office, Kenny shouldered his bag and hurried to the gravel parking lot, eager to get away.

His dark blue Jeep sat at the end of the lot, baking in the sun. As he unlocked the driver's door, a wave of hot air blasted him in the face. He slung his bag into the passenger seat and rolled down the window.

As he started to get in, he glanced through the windshield at the hood.

And let out a shout.

Two words had been scrawled across the hood. Written in slashes of thick, white paint.

YOU'RE DEAD.

Slowly Kenny backed out of the Jeep and moved to the hood. He could feel the anger building inside him as he gazed at the ugly words.

Ty. Ty did this.

In his mind's eye, Kenny saw the surly counselor striding from the parking lot just a moment earlier.

Carrying a can of *white* paint.

Kenny's fists clenched. Now *Ty is out to get me*, he realized.

Kenny glanced at the hood again. *YOU'RE DEAD*. The angry words had blistered in the sun.

He might be able to wash them off, but he knew the threat would never go away. Not unless he did something about it—now.

After slamming the door so hard he rocked the car, Kenny sprinted back across the parking lot and raced to the office building. He flung open the screen door and burst into the hall just as Ty emerged from Craig's office.

"Are you happy now?" Kenny shouted.

Ty only had time for a startled glance before Kenny was on him. "Are you happy now?" he repeated. He shoved Ty back and slammed him against the wall. "Was painting that crazy threat enough? Or do you have more sick plans up your sleeve?"

"Huh? What are you talking about?" Ty began to push himself away from the wall.

Kenny shoved him back. "Don't play dumb, okay? You've been on my case since day one. I know you did it!"

"Did what?" Ty cried, cradling his damaged hand protectively against his chest.

Kenny grabbed him by the shoulders and pinned him to the wall. Craig came bursting out of his office and yanked Kenny away. "What is going on?" he demanded.

"You're asking *me?*" Ty shouted. He straightened up and glared at Kenny. "Ask the nutcase here!"

Craig turned to Kenny. "Well?"

"Ty knows what's going on," Kenny told him, breathing hard. "He painted a sick message on the hood of my car."

"Are you *crazy?*" Ty snarled. "I've been painting cabins for two days. You think I have time to paint your car? I don't even know which car is yours."

"I *saw* you—coming out of the parking lot five minutes ago. With a can of paint!" Kenny shouted.

"Right—I had to go buy more." Ty pointed to a large can sitting against the wall. "Check it out. It's not even opened yet."

"You're a liar!" Kenny shrieked, advancing on him.

Ty jumped aside and crouched into a fighter's pose. "Watch it," he warned. "I can take you with one hand."

Craig stepped between them. "Enough!" he ordered. "Whatever's going on, you'd better end it right now. Or you both don't need to show up tomorrow."

Kenny glared at Ty. "Okay, you got my car," he declared, still breathing hard. "We're even. Okay?"

"Even? You don't know what *even* is." Ty's lip

curled in a menacing sneer. "But you'll find out. You can count on it."

In his bedroom Saturday afternoon, Kenny punched Jade's phone number in California and crossed his fingers. The phone rang once... twice... kept on ringing. On the twentieth ring, Kenny hung up.

Kenny had been calling since he got home the day before. He missed her. He needed to talk to her. Jamming his hands in his pockets, he paced to his desk, then back to the phone on the bedside table. To the window. Back to the phone.

He reached for the phone, then shook his head. Stupid, he thought. I can't keep calling every two minutes.

Restless and angry, he paced to the window again and gazed outside. His Jeep stood in the driveway, still wet from the quick wash he had given it. Some white paint remained, but at least the words were smeared.

Kenny still didn't know whether to believe Ty when he said he hadn't done it. But if Ty didn't paint that message, then who did?

Vincent? Maybe. Vincent was still angry with him. And he definitely put that snake in my bed even though he wouldn't admit it.

But Melly could have done it too, Kenny realized. She had had plenty of time. And she was so upset—upset enough to do this?

Kenny closed his eyes, picturing Melly scratching her face, scratching it . . . scratching it.

Kenny felt a pang of guilt. I was really mean to her, he told himself. I should give her a call. Apologize for the way I talked to her. I owe her that, no matter what.

Crossing to the desk, he found the wrinkled slip of paper with her address and phone number. He smoothed it out on the bedside table, then picked up the phone and dialed.

After two rings a piercing shriek blasted his ear. Then came a recorded voice. "The number you have dialed has been changed," it announced. "No further information is available."

Kenny hung up, checked the number, and dialed again. Same taped message. Weird.

So apologize in person, he told himself. I have her address. And I'm too restless to stay inside anyway.

Grabbing his car keys from the desk, Kenny hurried to the Jeep. Half an hour later he turned off the highway onto Main Street in Waynesbridge. After driving around a while, he finally found Aspen Road.

Number 136 needed some work. Weeds choked the dry grass, and the front steps sagged on one side. Except for the yellow-eyed cat staring suspiciously at him from the porch, the house looked deserted.

But as Kenny approached the house, he heard the faint sound of music from behind the door. He walked carefully up the sagging steps and rang the doorbell.

After a moment the door opened. A middle-aged woman with tired brown eyes gazed out at him from behind the screen door. "Yes?"

"Hi. I'm Kenny Klein," he said. "I'm from Shadyside Day Camp. Is Melly home?"

The woman gasped. "Are you *crazy*? Get *away* from here!" Her lips trembled and her eyes burned with anger. "Get away! Or I'll call the police!" she shrieked—and slammed the door in Kenny's face.

Chapter Seventeen

Kenny stumbled back—and stepped on the cat's tail. With a howl of outrage, it leaped up and streaked off the porch.

Shocked and confused, Kenny stared at the closed door. What was *that* about? he wondered. Did I get the wrong address?

He dug the paper from his pocket and checked it against the chipped black numbers next to the door: 136. He walked to the end of the porch and gazed at the street sign on the corner. Aspen Road.

Right address, he saw. So what's wrong? Do I look threatening or something?

He combed his fingers through his hair, smoothed the front of his shirt, and pushed the doorbell again.

The door stayed closed. But out of the corner

of his eye, Kenny saw the curtain twitch in the front window. "Hello?" he called. "Sorry to bother you. But maybe you misunderstood me. I'm looking for Melly Baker. I'm a friend of hers from Shadyside Camp."

"Get away from here!" the woman cried from inside the house. "You're sick—that's what you are. Sick! I'm calling the police!"

"But—"

"I have the phone in my hand and I'm punching 911!" she shouted.

And I'm gone, Kenny thought. He sprinted back to his Jeep and sped away. The woman might be nuts, but he didn't want to mess with the cops.

Turning the corner, he glanced out the window and caught a last glimpse of the house.

I know I had the right address, he thought. So what's going on?

"Okay, guys, there's been a switch in the schedule," Kenny announced at camp on Monday morning. "Craig is taking some of the older kids out on the nature trail. So you have archery again."

Graydon complained as Kenny led them to the archery range. The bowstrings were too hard to pull back, he griped. And the arrows fizzled out halfway to the targets.

Kenny barely listened.

While the guys are having archery, I can cut

out again and talk to Melly, he thought.

I have to talk to her, he thought. I have to apologize.

As he passed the cabins, he spotted Ty rolling paint onto a cabin wall. When he saw Kenny, he paused long enough to flash him a dirty look. Then he turned his back and began painting again.

Kenny shrugged and hurried on to the arts-and-crafts cabin. Inside, Debra was helping her group of girls make bird feeders out of cardboard milk cartons.

Melly was nowhere in sight.

Before Kenny could ask Debra about her, one of the girls dropped a bag of birdseed.

The girls started squealing and giggling and tossing handfuls of birdseed at each other.

Kenny decided he'd better not bother Debra. Melly is obviously not here anyway, he told himself.

Where could she be?

Turning away, he started back toward the archery range. As he passed the cabins again, he saw the paint roller in its tray next to an open paint can. But Ty had left.

He must be taking a break, Kenny decided. Maybe that's what Melly's doing.

And I know just where she would go.

Cutting away from the main path, Kenny took the one that led down to the lake. She's always hanging out there, he thought. It's where I first saw her. And she was out there that night I jumped off the rock. She loves the lake.

That's where I'll find her.

As the path opened up, Kenny stopped and gazed along the shoreline. Down at the far end, he thought he caught a glimpse of yellow. Someone in a staff uniform?

He shaded his eyes from the sun. "Melly! Melly, is that you?" he called.

The figure didn't move.

Kenny shouted again.

The figure turned.

Kenny waved his arms over his head and shouted her name again.

But a sharp pain cut off his voice in mid-cry. A sharp, stabbing pain in his shoulder.

Kenny gasped and cried out. Tried to reach back.

The pain grew stronger. Hotter. His shoulder felt on fire.

Kenny gasped again. Have I been shot?

His knees wobbled. He started to fall.

Down . . . down . . . down into pain.

Rough sand grazed his face. His vision blurred.

And the pain spread, radiating in hot, agonizing circles.

I'm dead, he realized. Dead.

Kenny suddenly remembered those three grinning skulls.

Then the darkness closed in completely.

Chapter Eighteen

A woman's face peered down at Kenny, a worried expression in her eyes.

I've seen that face before, Kenny thought. He stared up at her, trying to remember.

"How are you feeling?" the woman asked.

The camp nurse! "Mrs. Gomez?" he murmured. His lips felt dry. "Am I in the infirmary?"

"Bingo." Mrs. Gomez smiled and moved away.

Two more faces appeared. Craig's and another man's. "This is Dr. Stewart, Kenny," Craig told him. "He took care of your shoulder."

Kenny licked his lips and swallowed. "So I guess I'm not dead."

"Far from it," the doctor assured him. "You passed out from the shock. But the arrow missed everything vital. You'll have a nasty bruise, but your shoulder will be okay."

"Arrow?" Kenny gasped.

The doctor nodded. "I got it out without doing any damage."

"Thanks. Thanks a lot." With Mrs. Gomez's help, Kenny sat up on the infirmary cot. His stomach lurched as a wave of dizziness washed over him.

Kenny clutched the edge of the cot and waited for it to pass. "Who shot me?" he asked as Mrs. Gomez handed him a cup of water.

Craig shook his head. "I wish I knew. We asked everybody. The archery instructors didn't see anyone. Ty and I talked to all the boys, but they didn't know anything, either."

Kenny took a sip of water. His stomach churned again, but not as badly.

"Your group is in the cabin having a snack," Craig told Kenny. He started to pat him on the shoulder, then pulled his hand back. "I'm going to call your parents."

"No, don't do that," Kenny protested. "They'll make too big a deal out of it if they get a phone call. I'd rather just tell them when I get home."

"Fine," Craig agreed. "But you stay here and rest for a while."

Kenny nodded and thanked them all again as they left the room. He took another drink of water. So far, so good. Maybe he wouldn't throw up after all.

He swung his legs over the side of the cot. He still felt a little shaky, but not enough to lie down again.

Why is this happening to me? he wondered.

Slowly, Kenny stood up. As he did, something slid from beneath him and slapped onto the floor.

He glanced down. The sudden head movement made him woozy, but his vision didn't blur. He could see just fine.

Lying at his feet were three cards with black skulls on them.

Vincent!

Why is Vincent trying to kill me? Just to make his card prediction come true? Is he that twisted?

Kenny took a long, deep breath. His shoulder ached, but the dizziness didn't return. He made his way out of the room and walked slowly down the hall and out of the building.

When he reached Cabin 5, the boys leaped from their bunks, shouting questions.

"Who did it?" Charlie asked.

"I don't know," Kenny replied. He glanced around and noticed Vincent staring at him intently. "Anyway, the doctor says I'm okay."

"I bet it hurts," Graydon mumbled through a mouthful of potato chips.

"You bet right," Kenny agreed. "But I'll live. Okay, guys, snack time's just about over, so pack up the garbage. Vincent, it's your turn to take it to the trash bin, right?"

"Right." Vincent held out a large plastic bag while the other boys tossed in apple cores and crumpled cellophane bags. Kenny held the door open for Vincent, then followed him outside.

"Wait a sec, Vincent," Kenny told him.

Vincent stopped.

"I know what you're trying to do," Kenny declared. "And I'm warning you you'd better stop."

"Huh?"

"You're trying to make the prediction of the Doom Teller cards come true," Kenny said. "That's why you keep leaving those three skull cards with me, right?"

"That's not true." Vincent slowly shook his head. "No way."

Kenny shifted impatiently. "Look, Vincent, they're *your* cards."

"Yeah, but—"

"And they turn up every time something happens to me," Kenny interrupted.

"But I don't have them anymore!" Vincent cried. "They're gone. I think someone took them that night—after the campfire."

Kenny stared at him hard. Vincent's blue eyes stared back from the mask, wide and innocent-looking.

I wish I could see his whole face, Kenny thought. Maybe it would help me figure out what he's thinking. Is he lying? Is he? Is Vincent really trying to kill me?

*   *   *

By lunchtime Kenny felt weak all over. His shoulder throbbed constantly. And after looking for Melly all morning, he still hadn't found her.

How come she's never around when I'm trying to find her? he wondered. I need to talk to her and straighten things out.

Sore and frustrated, Kenny told Craig he'd decided to leave. He lugged his duffel bag out to the Jeep, then climbed inside and turned the air conditioner on. As the air began to cool, he leaned his head against the steering wheel and thought about Melly.

Why couldn't I find her? Did what I say freak her out so much that she is hiding from me?

He changed his mind about going home. I'll go back to Melly's house in Waynesbridge, he decided. Maybe she's there right now.

Kenny stopped at a gas station on the Mill Road and filled the tank. Then he slipped a cassette into the player and drove back to the Aspen Road house in Waynesbridge.

The place looked the same—worn and deserted. The cat was curled on the porch next to a full water bowl. And the voice of a talk-show host chattered away behind the door.

Somebody's home, Kenny thought. He rang the bell and waited.

The same woman pulled open the door.

"Please don't call the cops. I'm not here to

make trouble," Kenny declared in a rush. "I'm just trying to find Melly Baker, and this is the address I got for her at camp. If she doesn't want to see me, okay. But could you just tell me if she's here?"

The woman's eyes narrowed in anger. "I don't know what kind of cruel joke you're playing!" she exclaimed bitterly. "But my daughter Melly is dead! She died when she was eight years old. She drowned at Shadyside Day Camp."

Chapter Nineteen

Melly . . . dead?

His mind whirling in confusion, Kenny drove through the winding streets of his neighborhood and pulled to a stop in the driveway. As he hauled his duffel from the Jeep, a figure stepped out from the shadows of the garage.

Kenny straightened up, his heart beginning to thud.

Ty Sullivan stood in the garage doorway.

As he slowly emerged from the shadows, Kenny's heart speeded up.

In his good hand, Ty gripped an aluminum baseball bat.

Just what I need, Kenny thought. He's come to get even. To get revenge.

Ty stepped forward and raised the bat.

Kenny tried not to flinch. Can I take him on with this wounded shoulder?

"Well . . . here you are," Ty muttered, narrowing his eyes at Kenny.

Kenny stared at the bat. It's mine, he realized. He's going to beat me up with my own baseball bat.

"This was in your driveway," Ty said. "I thought I better get it out of the way before somebody ran over it."

Ty tossed the bat into the side yard. "Listen, I came to talk," he declared. "I want to call a truce."

"Whoa." Kenny let his breath out in relief. "For a second, I thought you were going to use that bat to pound me into the ground."

Ty shook his head. "Pretty hard to do with a broken hand. But listen, I know you didn't slam that trunk lid on purpose. I guess I just freaked. I was really steamed."

"And afraid of losing your job," Kenny added.

"Yeah. I *thought* of all kinds of ways to get back at you," Ty admitted. "But I never did anything about them. You have to believe me. I didn't paint your car, okay? I can't stand working at camp every day, knowing somebody doesn't trust me."

"Forget about the car," Kenny told him. "I know you didn't do it."

"You mean it?"

Kenny nodded. "I shouldn't have jumped you like that. I was steamed, too, but not anymore. I'm ready for a truce."

Ty relaxed and leaned against the Jeep's front bumper. "So who do you think did it?" he asked, gesturing toward the hood.

Kenny shut the driver's door, shaking his head. "It might be one of the kids in my group."

"No kidding? Oh—that's right," Ty said. "You have the disturbed one."

"Yeah. Don't remind me." Kenny sighed. "I'm not positive he did it. So I don't want to say anything yet."

"Be sure to keep a close eye on him, especially on the canoe trip," Ty warned.

Right, Kenny thought. The camp had its second overnight tomorrow. This time it would be at the Conononka River north of Shadyside. They'd sleep in tents on the bank and early Tuesday morning they'd take a canoe trip downriver and have a picnic.

"I'd be glad to help watch him," Ty declared. "But I can't row. All I can do is sign out the canoes."

"That's okay. Craig might think I'm a wimp if I

tell him how much this kid creeps me out. And speaking of being creeped out," he added. "Wait until I tell you about Melly."

"Melly the Weird?" Ty joked.

Kenny told him about Melly's frightening reaction when he called it off with her. "And when I went to her house to apologize, this woman told me that Melly is dead!" he exclaimed. "That Melly drowned at Shadyside Camp when she was eight."

Ty glanced at him skeptically.

"That's what she said," Kenny insisted. "You want to drive to Waynesbridge with me and talk to her yourself?"

"No, I believe you," Ty told him. "But how come you're so surprised? I mean, Melly's a total psycho. Why shouldn't her whole family be nuts?"

Maybe Ty is right, Kenny decided. He thought of the way Melly came unglued yesterday. He remembered the shrill, bitter voice of the woman in Waynesbridge and the way she screamed at him.

Melly can't be dead, he thought.

But she's definitely crazy.

"We should get into our tents for lights out," Kenny told his group on the next night. "The canoe trip starts first thing in the morning."

"It's too early to go to sleep," Graydon

argued. He stabbed a hot dog onto his stick and held it over the campfire. "Besides, I'm still hungry."

"Okay. One more hot dog," Kenny told him. He rubbed his aching shoulder and glanced around. Several fires burned along the south bank of the Conononka River, where the Shadyside campers had pitched their tents. Beneath the crackling of the fire and the chattering voices, he could hear the steady sound of the flowing water.

Kenny rubbed his shoulder again. It was getting better. He just hoped paddling a canoe for an hour didn't do too much damage.

"Guess what?" Vincent's voice broke into Kenny's thoughts. "I got a new deck of Doom Teller cards."

Graydon gave him a challenging glance. "Ha. You said they were so special. You told us your grandfather gave them to you."

"He did," Vincent agreed. "He gave me another deck."

"Where did *he* get them?" Graydon demanded.

"It's a secret." Vincent pulled the deck of cards from his pocket. "Want to try again, Kenny?"

No way, Kenny thought.

"You're not scared, are you?" Vincent asked. His lips twisted in a weird grin. "I mean, you got the three skulls the last time, and you're still alive."

So far, Kenny thought.

"Besides, maybe your luck has changed." Vincent's eyes sparkled crazily. "Don't you want to find out?"

Kenny felt the other boys watching him. I can't say no, he thought. They'd wonder why. And I can't let on that Vincent frightens me. "Okay," he agreed. "Let's do it."

"Great." Vincent fanned the cards out. Kenny chose three and lay them facedown in the dirt.

Vincent set the deck aside and picked up the three cards. Slowly he turned them around for everyone to see.

Kenny had chosen the same cards.

Three black skulls.

Kenny stared at them, not sure what to say. The other boys stayed silent, hardly breathing. Their eyes flicked back and forth from Kenny's face to the cards.

"Hey." Graydon suddenly broke the silence. "Let me see those cards." Before Vincent could stop him, Graydon grabbed the deck and fanned it out. "Whoa!" he cried. "Check this out!"

Graydon turned all the cards over.

Kenny couldn't believe it. Every one of them had a black skull on it!

"Faker!" Graydon tossed the deck at Vincent.

The cards bounced off Vincent's chest. He threw his head back and shouted with laughter. His mask fluttered around his mouth and his eyes gleamed.

In Too Deep

The other boys exchanged glances. None of them joined in Vincent's laughter.

Kenny gazed at the dark river and shivered. He had a bad feeling about the canoe trip tomorrow.

Chapter Twenty

"**W**ow! Check out those speedboats!" Charlie cried as Kenny led the group onto the wooden dock the next morning. "I bet they can really fly!"

"Stay away from them," Ty warned. He stood at the end of the dock, signing off another group of kids. "They're only for adults."

"Ty's right," Kenny agreed. He gave an admiring glance to the silver-and-blue boats nosed up to the right side of the dock. The other group of campers had just paddled away, leaving three fiberglass canoes bumping gently against the pilings.

"Ready to take a trip?" Ty asked. "How's the shoulder?"

"Not too bad," Kenny told him. "I think I can make it."

"Good." Ty checked his list. "Okay, you have three canoes. Divide up—three, three, and two. Why don't you go with two of the kids?" he suggested. "That will save you some paddling."

"Good idea," Kenny agreed. He divided the boys into partners and checked to make sure their life jackets were on tight. He helped David, Vincent, and Dan into a canoe and pushed them off.

A few minutes later Ty steadied the second canoe and Kenny lowered himself into it. Then he helped Matthew and Simon down.

Matthew sat in front, Simon took the middle seat, and Kenny sat in the rear.

Ty gave the canoe a shove with his good hand. "You're off!" he shouted.

Kenny waved to Graydon and Charlie, who waited to get into the third canoe.

As Kenny and the boys paddled away from the dock, his shoulder throbbed slightly. But once their boat reached the middle of the river, the current took over and pulled them along much faster than he expected.

"This is great!" Matthew exclaimed. "I don't even see the first canoe. It must be flying!"

"Yeah," Simon agreed. "Think we can go the whole trip without paddling?"

Kenny laughed. "We might have to work a little when we reach the bend," he said, pointing ahead to where the river curved. "We don't want to beach this thing."

As the boys pointed at places on the banks and argued about how fast they were moving, Kenny began to enjoy himself.

The river was cool in the early morning, and the bugs hadn't come out yet. The air smelled fresh and sweet.

He turned back. No sign of the third canoe, but he didn't worry. That's what the speedboats were for—so other counselors could patrol the river and make sure no one got into trouble.

When they reached the bend, Kenny and the boys dipped their paddles into the water and eased the canoe around the wide curve.

"Piece of cake!" Kenny declared as the river straightened out ahead of them.

"I'm thirsty," Simon declared.

Kenny bent forward to open the small cooler resting between his feet. As he pulled out two juice boxes, he paused, listening.

What was that buzzing sound? A mosquito?

The buzzing grew louder. Definitely not a mosquito, Kenny thought.

The buzzing quickly became a roar. Kenny glanced over his shoulder.

A sleek silver speedboat rounded the bend and slapped through the water, heading for the canoe.

Hey—what's going on? It's moving way too fast! Kenny thought. Once it passes us, we'll turn over in its wake!

The canoe rocked as Kenny turned and waved his arms. "Slow down!" he shouted to the driver. "You'll turn us over! Kill the engine!"

The roar grew louder. The speedboat slashed closer.

Who's driving that thing? Kenny wondered angrily. The guy's a maniac!

The glare of the sun on the water and the metallic silver boat made it almost impossible to see. Kenny rose halfway to his feet and shaded his eyes.

A jolt of fear raced up his spine as he finally focused on the driver, wearing a red-and-white ski mask!

"Vincent!" Simon shrieked.

It can't be! Kenny thought. Vincent left before we did!

The speedboat roared closer, slapping over the water, a silver blur.

"He isn't going to stop!" Matthew screamed. The canoe rocked dangerously. "He's going to hit us!"

An image of the speedboat's blades flashed into Kenny's mind. Sharp as daggers, they'd slice through the lifejackets. Cut flesh into shreds. Churn blood and skin and water into a hideous mix.

"Jump!" Kenny screamed.

Too late.

The speedboat was on them.

In the split second before it rammed the canoe, Kenny locked his eyes on the driver's.

Bright blue eyes, glittering with excitement.

With a loud crash, the speedboat plowed into the canoe.

Kenny flew into the air, his ears ringing with the whine of the motor. He caught a glimpse of an orange life jacket . . . of Matthew's terrified face flying past him. He thought he heard Simon, shrieking in terror.

Then Kenny plunged into the river. The water closed over his head, blotting out everything.

Chapter Twenty-one

K enny broke the surface with a loud gasp. Water streamed from his hair into his eyes, blinding him for a second. Bobbing in the life jacket, he shook the water from his face and glanced around frantically for Matthew and Simon.

The capsized canoe floated nearby, dented and scraped from the collision. As Kenny swam toward it, he spotted two patches of bright orange near the south bank of the river.

Matthew and Simon, swimming to the shore.

Relief flooded through Kenny as the two boys stood in the shallow water. They're safe, he thought, watching them scramble up the muddy bank. The blades didn't get them.

Kenny grabbed hold of the battered canoe and

leaned his head against it, catching his breath. Somehow, Vincent managed to get back to the dock and get the speedboat, he thought. But how? Why didn't Ty see him?

The current flowed strongly, pulling him with it. He started to kick toward shore—then suddenly stopped, frozen in fear.

The speedboat's roar filled the air again. Coming closer.

Kenny's heart raced as he saw the silver boat slicing through the water, heading straight at him.

Vincent turned it around! he saw. He's not finished. He's coming back to get me!

Terrified, Kenny dived beneath the water. And bobbed straight up again. The life jacket! he realized. It won't let me dive.

With the roar of the motor growing louder and louder, Kenny struggled frantically with the life jacket belt. His fingers slipped. Water lapped into his mouth. He choked and coughed, then finally caught hold of the belt again and ripped it loose.

The silver boat bounced across the water. Kenny shrugged the jacket off one shoulder.

The boat drew closer. As Kenny struggled to get the jacket off his other shoulder, he saw Vincent's eyes again. Wide-open and gleaming with excitement, they zeroed in on Kenny like lasers.

It's too late, Kenny told himself. I'll never get

far enough under in time! Those blades are going to slice me in half!

As the boat sped dangerously close, Kenny yanked the jacket free, swung his arm back, and heaved the life jacket straight at Vincent's face.

Vincent ducked. The boat swerved. Just missed Kenny.

Kenny tried to dive under as the boat sped by, but its wake knocked him on his side. Churning water rushed into his mouth and nose. He floundered and thrashed, then finally righted himself, spitting water and gasping for air.

The sound of the motor roared in his ears. So close. Too close! He's coming right back around!

Kenny felt a flash of terror as he saw Vincent aim the sleek little boat at him again. No time to swim. No time to dive. Nothing to do but scream.

But then he suddenly realized something—the boat wasn't speeding anymore. Vincent had tried to spin it in a tight turn, and he wasn't a good enough pilot.

The boat had slowed down.

This is my chance, Kenny told himself. My only chance!

Before the boat could pick up speed and go flat out again, Kenny propelled himself through the water and hooked his arms over its side.

Vincent didn't notice.

Groaning with the effort, Kenny hauled himself over the side and tumbled onto the deck.

Kenny landed behind Vincent. The boy turned, his eyes wide with surprise.

Kenny rolled to his knees and jumped up. With a shout of fury, he leaped to the front of the boat and grabbed Vincent by the arm.

Vincent struggled to jerk free, snarling and pulling and kicking out.

Kenny held on tight, trying to dodge the blows. He kept stretching his arm, trying to reach the key and turn the motor off. But Vincent fought wildly, slamming his fist into the side of Kenny's neck and battering his shins with both feet.

He's so strong, Kenny thought. How can such a skinny little kid be so strong?

Except he isn't skinny anymore, Kenny noticed as he danced backward out of range of Vincent's foot. His arm feels thick. Almost flabby. And what about his neck?

Vincent's ski mask had ridden up during the struggle, exposing the front part of his neck. The same part Kenny had seen before.

But now, no wormy scars crisscrossed the throat. All Kenny could see was smooth, pale skin.

Wait a sec, Kenny thought. Who is this? Who am I fighting?

The boy swung his arm again, aiming a fist at Kenny's head. Kenny caught hold of his wrist and jerked him forward.

The move took the boy by surprise. He stumbled a couple of steps, then fell to his knees.

Kenny lurched forward and shut the motor off. Then he whirled around and hauled the boy to his feet.

"Who are you?" he cried. The boy struggled to break free again. But Kenny caught him by the shoulders and jerked him backward.

Gripping him tightly with one hand, Kenny grabbed hold of the mask—and ripped it over the boy's head.

"Huh? You?" Kenny cried.

Chapter Twenty-two

C ompletely stunned, Kenny stared into the furious blue eyes of Graydon Boyce.

Graydon glared back at him.

"Why?" Kenny demanded. "Why did you try to kill us?"

"I didn't try to kill *them*," Graydon snarled. "Just you."

Kenny flinched at the hate and fury in the boy's voice.

"Just you, Kenny," Graydon repeated. "You were the one I wanted to kill. Because you deserve to die."

A short while later Kenny, Craig, and Graydon stood near the boat dock, waiting for Graydon's mother to arrive and take him home.

Graydon had seethed in silence as Kenny

piloted the boat back to the dock. But when Craig arrived and began asking questions, Graydon erupted in anger.

"This whole camp is full of dweebs!" he declared. "Charlie and I were supposed to get into the canoe. And all of a sudden he started to puke. So Ty decided to find somebody to take him home. And they left me alone on the dock. With the key in the boat," he added with a sneer.

"But why did you come after me?" Kenny demanded, still shaking. "What did I do, Graydon?"

"Ha. As if you didn't know!" Graydon snapped.

"I don't!" Kenny insisted.

Graydon's face reddened. "You spent all your time with that masked freak!"

"Vincent?" Kenny frowned in confusion. "I don't get it. I didn't spend lots of time with him."

"You did too. You always let him walk with you. You'd pat him on the shoulder and talk to him all the time. I saw you—after breakfast, and outside the cabin, and at the overnight," Graydon declared. "You didn't care about anybody but him!"

Kenny glanced at Craig again. Craig shook his head. Don't argue with him, he seemed to say.

"Poor Vincent. Be nice to the weirdo. Give the freak a chance!" Graydon complained. "Well, what about what *me*? You didn't care about me. Just Vincent. You ruined my summer . . . so I paid you back." He bared his teeth and made a hissing sound. "Ssssnap!"

"Huh? The snake?" Kenny asked in surprise. "*You* put that snake in my bed?"

"Duh . . . yeah!" Graydon replied sarcastically. "But that didn't work, so I decided to freak you out some more. I painted your car. And then I plugged you with that arrow. Ha ha. That was so cool!"

Kenny didn't answer. I can't believe this! he thought.

"Then I bought a mask just like Vincent's. I wasn't sure when I'd use it. But I got my chance today." Graydon burst out laughing. "You should have seen your face when I was coming at you!"

Craig took Graydon's arm and walked him to a car that had just pulled up near the dock. Kenny watched as he helped the boy inside. He stood talking to the driver for a moment, then returned to Kenny.

"Whew!" Craig ran a hand through his hair. "That boy is something else!"

"Yeah. I still can't believe he did all those things to me," Kenny declared.

"I warned you that he was disturbed," Craig said.

Kenny stared at him, completely shocked. "Huh? Graydon?"

Craig nodded. "Didn't you read his profile? It described how troubled he is."

"But . . . what about Vincent?" Kenny stammered.

"What do you mean? The poor kid was in a bad accident," Craig replied. "That's all we know about him."

"Oh, man," Kenny murmured. "I thought for sure *he* was the troubled one. He acts so weird sometimes."

"Vincent is probably just self-conscious. Anyway, it's over now. Matthew and Simon are fine. They didn't even want to go home." Craig clapped Kenny on the shoulder. "Why don't you take it easy for a while? Dry off. Then you can take one of the boats down to the picnic area."

Kenny thanked him, then walked to the river's edge. He found a smooth, flat boulder and sat down. He kicked off his shoes and squeezed the water from his socks.

The sun floated higher now, and its heat began to dry his hair and clothes. He shut his eyes and listened to the river and the sound of the speedboats bumping against the dock.

He still felt stunned. It had been Graydon all along, not Vincent.

I have to apologize to the kid, he decided. After all, I accused him of some pretty bad stuff. And he didn't do a thing.

Don't waste any more time, Kenny told himself. Go down to the picnic area and talk to Vincent now.

Kenny straightened up and felt his socks. Still wet. He stuck a hand in one of his sneakers. Totally soggy. Barefoot is better, he decided. He balled up the socks and shoved them inside the sneakers.

Something caught his eye as he stood up.

A flash of color, out in the middle of the river.

Kenny cupped a hand over his eyes and gazed across the sparkling water.

He noticed a spot of yellow. It looked like some kind of cloth.

A shirt, that's what it is, Kenny realized. Bright yellow, like the camp staff wears.

Squinting hard against the sun's glare, Kenny suddenly gasped.

A body!

There's a body out there, floating facedown in the river!

Blond hair floating on the surface.

Blond hair spread out on the water like pale yellow seaweed.

Melly's hair!

Chapter Twenty-three

"**M**elly!" Kenny cupped his hands and screamed her name. "Melly!"

Melly's body spun in a circle, then continued to float as the current pulled it downriver.

Kenny dropped his shoes and plunged down the muddy bank. He started to dive into the river, then stopped. Take a boat, he told himself. It will be much faster.

He scrambled up the bank and dashed to the dock, where the speedboats were tied.

Is she alive? he wondered.

Is there a chance she's still alive?

It's my fault, Kenny thought. She said she couldn't live without me.

Kenny jumped into the metallic blue speedboat. He settled himself in the driver's seat and turned the key.

The motor kicked on with a roar, churning the water into a white froth. As Kenny reached over to untie the rope, the motor began to choke. The choke turned to a sputter.

"No!" Kenny cried. The motor sputtered again. Then it died.

Kenny turned the key.

The motor didn't even groan.

Kenny checked the gas gauge. Empty.

With a cry of frustration, Kenny scrambled out of the blue boat and into the shiny silver one that Graydon had tried to kill him with.

The key was gone.

Kenny pounded the wheel, feeling desperate. He had to get to Melly! He'd have to swim after all.

As he started to climb out of the boat, he suddenly remembered. He'd stuck the key in his pocket after he brought Graydon back.

Kenny dug the key out and sank back into the driver's seat. His hand shook as he tried to stick the key into the ignition. He missed twice, then finally slid it in.

The motor roared to life. And kept roaring.

Kenny untied the rope and pushed away from the dock. The minute he cleared it, he aimed the boat downriver and jammed it into high gear.

The boat took off with a burst of speed, slamming Kenny back against the seat. Water sprayed over the bow and misted his face. The trees on the banks flashed past in a blur of green. Kenny could feel the river underneath him, slapping against the bottom of the boat as he pushed it to go faster.

The river spread out in front of him, wide and empty.

No, not empty!

The speck of yellow was still there, bobbing gently as the river pulled it along.

Keeping his gaze pinned on the flash of yellow, Kenny roared down the river. Melly is still floating, he thought. Maybe I can save her. Maybe she is alive.

Kenny could see Melly's hair floating around her head. He cut back on the throttle, steering carefully.

As he drew closer, he turned the wheel and eased the boat alongside Melly. He shifted into idle, then stretched over the side, trying to snag the back of Melly's shirt.

The boat rose and dipped. It began to drift away.

Kenny leaned farther over the edge, stretching his hand out. The boat tilted with his weight.

Kenny gritted his teeth and reached out again. His fingers finally caught the shoulder of Melly's shirt.

He gave her a tug, gasping with the effort.

Kenny caught her by the arm. It felt heavy. Lifeless.

She's dead, he thought. Drowned. I can't believe it!

As he started to haul her into the boat, Melly's body suddenly jerked. Her head rose up.

With water streaming down her face, she opened her eyes. Then she clamped cold fingers to the back of Kenny's neck and grinned at him.

Chapter Twenty-four

Kenny jerked back, uttering a startled cry.

Melly's sharp nails raked his neck. Then her fingers dug into his arm.

"You're alive!" Kenny cried. "I can't believe it!"

Melly slowly shook her head. Her fingers dug into his arm.

"Climb in!" Kenny demanded. "You're alive! You're okay!"

"No, Kenny," Melly whispered, water pouring from her mouth. "You're wrong. I'm not okay. I'm not alive."

"Huh?"

"I'm not alive," Melly repeated. "I'm dead."

Kenny gaped at her. "What are you saying?"

"I died a long time ago," Melly whispered.

"When I was eight years old."

Kenny gasped. He pictured the woman in Waynesbridge, telling him about her daughter. How she died when she was eight.

But that wasn't Melly! he told himself. It couldn't have been!

"Don't you remember me?" Melly cried.

"Remember you?" Kenny asked. "I never met you until the first day of day camp!"

"That's not true," Melly replied. "Think, Kenny. Remember back to when *you* went to Shadyside Camp. The summer you were nine."

"I . . . I don't understand," he stammered.

"You were nine and I was eight. And I had such a crush on you," Melly told him. "Such a crush it was painful. I couldn't wait to get to camp each morning so I could see you again. I spent all my time watching you. Don't you even remember me?"

"No, I . . . I'm sorry," Kenny replied.

"I know someone you'll remember!" Melly tightened her cold grip on his arm and pulled herself closer. "Tyler! That mean counselor, remember him?"

A face flashed into Kenny's mind. A square face, with hard eyes and bushy eyebrows that wiggled like caterpillars when he frowned.

Ty Gruman. I *do* remember, Kenny thought. He was a counselor one of the summers I was here. Nobody liked him. We called him Tyler

Grumpman. I remember reading that he died a few years ago.

But Melly thinks he's still here. She has him mixed up with Ty Sullivan. They're two different people!

"You do remember, don't you?" Melly asked. "Ty was so cruel. He made me go canoeing even though I felt sick. I cried and begged not to go, but he wouldn't listen!"

"But it's not the same Ty," Kenny insisted. "It's not the same guy!"

"And then my canoe tipped over and hit me on the head. And . . . I drowned!" she cried. "How could you forget that, Kenny? How could you forget a girl drowning?"

"Because I never knew!" Kenny declared. "I guess they never told us. I guess they didn't want to upset us."

But it couldn't have happened! he told himself. Melly is alive. She's so crazy she imagined the whole thing.

"I waited for you, Kenny," Melly continued. "I watched you every day—from the other side. That's how I knew you'd come back."

Kenny glanced around. If only someone would show up, he thought. I could really, really use some help here.

Melly tugged on his arm, her fingers digging in painfully. "Look at me, Kenny. Look at me!"

Kenny turned his gaze back to her face.

Melly smiled, the same smile that he hadn't been able to resist the first time he saw her.

But the smile didn't excite him now.

It terrified him.

"I borrowed this girl's body from the cemetery so you would like me," Melly told him softly.

Kenny couldn't speak. A body from a cemetery? What was she talking about?

Melly licked a drop of water from her lips. Her eyes gazed at him hungrily. "You do like me—don't you?" she asked, her voice dropping to a throaty purr.

Kenny still couldn't speak. He didn't know what to think anymore.

"I hope you like me," she murmured. "Because you're going to come with me now."

Kenny swallowed. "Come with you? What do you mean? Where?"

"You'll see." Melly raised her other arm and grasped his neck with icy fingers. "You're going to stay with me—forever."

Before Kenny could react, Melly tightened her grip and yanked him over the side of the boat.

Chapter Twenty-five

Kenny barely had time to take a breath before he hit the water. As he tried to twist his body and kick back to the surface, he felt Melly's hands grasping him.

Pulling him down.

Holding him under.

She's trying to drown me! he realized in horror. That's what she meant when she said I would stay with her forever.

Kenny thrashed hard, kicking and twisting. Struggling to get up to the surface.

But he couldn't break Melly's grip. With her arms locked around his neck, she pulled him deeper.

She's so strong! Kenny thought.

Inhumanly strong.

Kenny grabbed hold of her arms. Dug his nails in. Tried to pry them loose.

Melly's muscles tightened like iron.

Kenny felt his eyes begin to bulge. His heart thundered and his lungs ached for air.

Don't do it! he told himself. Don't let your breath out or you'll die.

Desperate for air, Kenny rolled hard, trying to shake Melly loose. But she rolled with him, her arms clamped tight around his neck.

A thin stream of bubbles began to flow from Kenny's mouth. He couldn't stop it. He couldn't hold it back. A jolt of panic shot through him—when he took a breath, his lungs would fill with water!

The stream of bubbles continued to seep from his mouth. Frantic now, he rolled to his back.

As Melly rolled with him, her body swung sideways. Kenny brought his knees up, then kicked her viciously in the stomach.

Melly's arms dropped away as she opened her mouth in a silent scream.

Kenny quickly twisted around, his lungs ready to explode. He kicked out one more time, pulled with his arms—and shot up to the surface.

His head broke through the water. Coughing and choking, he dragged in breath after breath of air.

His legs and arms felt like lead. His head spun, making him dizzy. He couldn't stop shivering.

He took a shuddering breath and glanced around.

The boat had drifted way downstream. Leave it, Kenny told himself. The shore is closer.

He turned and began to swim toward the shore.

And screamed as a hand clamped around his ankle.

Kenny kicked with his free foot, but Melly grabbed that one too. Then she began to pull.

"No!" Kenny screamed. "Nooo!"

I can't fight her again, he thought in a panic. I'm too exhausted. She'll kill me this time.

As he struggled to stay above the water, Kenny heard a noise. A distant buzz, getting closer.

He turned to see a blue speedboat racing downstream, bouncing over the water at high speed. As it drew closer, Kenny recognized the pilot. Blond hair. A glint of gold in his eyebrow.

Ty!

"Help!" Kenny waved his arms and screamed. "Ty! Help me!"

Melly let go of Kenny's ankles and grabbed hold of a leg with both her hands.

Kenny kicked out with his other leg. "Nooo!" he screamed again. "Ty!"

Melly twisted her fingers into the back of Kenny's shirt.

Bad move, Kenny thought. She'd left his arms and legs free. He doubled up, almost into a ball, then flipped over.

Melly somersaulted over him, her hands breaking loose from his shirt. Kenny kicked both feet forward, into the back of her head.

"Ty!" Kenny spun around and pulled himself through the water toward the oncoming boat.

Ty swerved the boat sideways and slowed it to idle.

"Get me out of here—fast!" Kenny choked out, stretching an arm up. "She ... she's trying to drown me!"

Ty clamped the fingers of his good hand around Kenny's wrist and hauled him out of the river.

Kenny rolled to his back on the deck. "Thanks," he gasped. "You saved my life. She was pulling me under. She would have killed me."

"Who?" Ty gazed around, a confused expression on his face. "Who are you talking about, Kenny? There's no one else out here."

Chapter Twenty-six

"**S**he was with me. In the river," Kenny gasped. "Didn't you see her?"

"See who?"

"Melly!" Kenny struggled shakily to his feet and glanced all around.

Ty was right.

No one else out there.

Melly had disappeared.

"I don't get it," Kenny declared. His teeth chattered from the cold. "Melly was trying to drag me under. To drown me. You had to see us splashing around out there."

"Sure, I saw a lot of water splashing," Ty agreed. "But when I got close, I didn't see anybody but you."

Kenny hugged himself. He couldn't stop shivering.

"Listen, man, you're shaking like crazy," Ty said. "I'm taking you back to shore." He turned the boat and headed toward a sunny cove on the south bank.

"Melly was out there with me!" Kenny argued as they sped across the water. "She said she was dead. She said she died when she was eight. But she came back—and she's been waiting for me."

"Kenny . . ."

"That's what she said!" Kenny cried. "She's dead, but she borrowed a body—so I would like her. And I did, at first. But when I changed my mind, she decided to drown me—so we could be together. She was strong—so strong!"

Kenny shivered violently, and Ty gave him a worried glance. "You're not making any sense," he said.

"I know it sounds crazy—but it happened!" Kenny declared. "I can't explain it. All I know is that Melly's out here in the river somewhere!" He tightened his arms around himself as another violent shiver shook his body.

Ty nosed the boat into the cove and tied it to a thick log that jutted into the water. Leaving the boat running, he hoisted Kenny over the side. Then he led him to a dry, sunny patch of ground on the shore.

Kenny collapsed onto the dirt, gasping and shaking.

"Don't move," Ty told him. "Just lie there,

okay? You're in shock. I'll go get help." He glanced into the trees behind them. "The trail is up that way. Some of the groups are hiking on it. I'll meet up with somebody faster than if I take the boat all the way back to the dock or down to the picnic."

"Right." Kenny clamped his lips together, trying to stop his teeth from chattering.

"So just lie here in the sun," Ty repeated. "Don't move. I'll be back with some help real fast."

Kenny nodded.

Ty patted his shoulder and took off through the trees.

Kenny curled into a ball and tried to stop shaking. After a few minutes, the shivers grew less violent. He rolled to his back and closed his eyes.

The sun beat down, heating his skin and slowly drying his clothes. He felt tired to the bone. Warm. Drowsy.

A speedboat roared nearby, filling the air with a loud buzz. Kenny tried to shut it out. He wanted to sleep.

He opened his eyes—and yelped in fear.

Vincent's masked face loomed over him, his blue eyes glittering. "You're coming with me, Kenny."

"What . . . what's going on?" Kenny started to sit up, but the boy pushed him back. "Vincent, what are you doing here?"

"I came to get you. You're coming with me," he repeated. His voice sounded strange. Weak and raspy.

Kenny tried to sit again, but Vincent shoved him down. Then he raised his arm.

Kenny gasped.

Vincent held a knife. A razor-sharp butcher knife, its long blade gleaming in the sun.

"I wanted to do it neatly with a drowning," Vincent declared. "But I guess I'll have to do it the messy way."

With a furious cry, Vincent plunged the knife toward Kenny's chest.

Chapter Twenty-seven

Kenny jerked his body to the side.

The knife sank into dirt up to the hilt, an inch from Kenny's back.

"Nooo!" Vincent screamed in disappointment and fury. He yanked the knife out and raised it over his head. "You're coming with me!"

Kenny shot up—and jammed his head into Vincent's stomach. He locked his fingers around the boy's wrist.

Vincent screamed again. A wave of foul breath blasted from his mouth into Kenny's face.

Kenny almost gagged as Vincent screamed again, struggling and kicking. Trying to get loose.

Kenny bent the boy's wrist back. Farther. Farther.

Shrieking in pain, Vincent finally opened his fingers.

The knife dropped to the ground. Vincent dived for it—but Kenny beat him to it. He snatched it up and hurled it into the trees.

Before Kenny could move, Vincent leaped onto his back and flattened him to the ground. The boy's fingers clutched Kenny's head, ripping at his hair. Digging into the side of his neck.

He's going for my throat, Kenny thought in terror. He's crazy! Totally insane!

Kenny rolled again. Vincent rolled with him, then scrambled to his knees and stretched his fingers toward Kenny's throat.

Kenny knocked the boy's hands aside, grabbed hold of his mask, and ripped it over his head.

Kenny opened his mouth in a scream of horror.

The face of a corpse stared down at him.

Green mold covered the skull. Its eyes oozed a thick yellow fluid that dripped down its jaws. Decaying lips peeled back over blackened teeth in a hideous smile.

"It's me, honey," the corpse declared. A wave of putrid air wafted from its mouth. "It's Melly."

"Uhh . . . no!" Kenny gasped. "You can't be."

"But I am," the corpse insisted. "I borrowed *two* bodies from the cemetery. This one is in bad shape, I know. And it's getting worse. But the other one—the pretty one—couldn't be with you all the time."

Kenny's stomach churned as the foul breath nearly smothered him.

"And I had to be close to you, honey. Every minute of every day," Melly whispered. "So I decided to be one of the campers in your group. And I used this body to do it."

It can't be true, Kenny thought.

Images of the past few days flashed through his mind. Vincent going to wash off the red paint, then Melly showing up. Vincent leaving the campfire, then Melly stopping by a couple of minutes later. Melly standing by the lake right after Vincent had walked away from the cabin.

It's true, Kenny realized. I never saw Vincent and Melly in the same place at the same time. It was always one or the other. Never together.

"I had to be close to you," Melly repeated. "I know you understand."

The mold-covered skull leaned forward. Its foul breath filled his nose. Its face loomed closer—until it pressed its cold, rotting lips against Kenny's mouth.

Chapter Twenty-eight

Kenny gagged.

The wet, cold lips pressed hard against his. He could feel the rotting teeth behind the lips.

"Get away!" he gasped, gagging again.

"Don't be like that," Melly begged. A small chunk of her bottom lip dropped off. "Don't you understand how long I waited? I have to be close to you!"

Kenny scrambled back, wiping his mouth with the back of his hand. His stomach churned at the sight of her. The smell of her.

"Please, Kenny, come with me!" Melly urged. "We can be so happy."

She reached for him again, but Kenny leaped to his feet. He wanted to run, but he forced himself not to.

I have to get rid of her, he thought. She'll find a way to kill me if I don't! She's dead, and she wants me dead too!

Before Melly could make another move, Kenny leaned down and hauled her to her feet. She started to smile. She thought he was hugging her.

No way, Kenny thought. Holding her tight, he began dragging her toward the river.

"What are you doing?" she cried. "Kenny!"

I'm putting you back where you belong, Kenny thought. You died when you were eight. Now it's time to die again.

"Kenny!" Melly begged, twisting in his arms. Her decayed body weighed almost nothing, but she struggled and kicked with inhuman strength.

Kenny held on, forcing himself not to choke from the smell, not to feel the cold, wet flesh in his hands. He kept going, staggering as she kicked and fought.

When he reached the river's edge, he saw her speedboat—Vincent's speedboat—engine chugging. He raised the body over his head—and heaved it into the air.

Shrieking in horror, Melly plunged into the water, into the whirring, razor-sharp blades of the speedboat.

The blades sliced the body's head from its neck. The skull flew up, then splashed down—and sank like a stone.

The blades spun, slicing off an arm. A leg.

Another arm. Blood spurted into the air, spattering the boat and the riverbank. Shreds of decayed flesh rained down on the water, floating on the surface like pieces of confetti.

Black smoke began to spew from the motor. Its whine turned to a growl. As a chunk of bone rattled against the blades, the motor finally died.

Silence now.

Kenny dropped to his knees, dizzy and sick. He lowered his head and waited for the feeling to pass.

Slowly he raised his head and took a deep breath. The smoke had drifted away. The sour smell of death faded.

Only leaves floated on the river's surface now.

"Are you gone, Melly?" he murmured. "Are you finally gone?"

As the water lapped quietly against the bank, he heard a faint voice pleading with him. "Don't forget me this time, Kenny. Please don't forget me!"

"Don't worry," Kenny muttered. He rose to his feet and turned away. "I won't."

About R.L. Stine

R.L. Stine is the best-selling author in America. He has written more than one hundred scary books for young people, all of them bestsellers.

His series include *Fear Street, Ghosts of Fear Street,* and the *Fear Street Sagas*.

Bob grew up in Columbus, Ohio. Today he lives in New York City with his wife, Jane, his son, Matt, and his dog, Nadine.

Don't Miss FEAR STREET® SENIORS
Episode Three!

THE THIRST

Senior year is a killer.

Especially this year at Shadyside High. The first day of school and already the prediction that the seniors will die is coming true.

A cheerleader is dead—drained of all her blood. Could this be the work of a vampire? A psycho killer?

Dana Palmer and her twin sister Deirdre need to find out soon. Because all signs show that they will be the next to die.